"NICK, NEXT TIME LET'S MEET AT THE HOSpital," Mercy suggested breathlessly.

"Don't you worry. We're gonna meet in lots of places, *chère*," Nick assured her as he turned the crystal knob of her bedroom door. "Places where you've never been. I promise you that."

"Where are you going? Wait—" Mercy ordered, but the master of innuendo was already out of her bedroom and on his way out the front door.

Quickly, she pulled on a pair of jeans and ran after him. She had to catch Nick and make sure he understood she'd only agreed to help with the fundraiser, no more. She flew down the staircase after him. "Nick, wait. You can't just turn your back and walk away. I'm not through with you!" she called as she burst through the door.

Stopping on the bottom porch step, his shirt still open, Nick turned. "That makes us even, *chère*. 'Cause I'm not through with you either. Not near through."

He swept back up the steps and pulled her against his bare chest in one motion. Shamelessly he snugged her body next to his, touching her everywhere. The rush of sensation was incredible and Mercy leaned into the embrace, admitting to herself that she'd wanted this kiss since yesterday. . . .

WHAT ARE *LOVESWEPT* ROMANCES?

They are stories of true romance and touching emotion. We believe those two very important ingredients are constants in our highly sensual and very believable stories in the LOVESWEPT line. Our goal is to give you, the reader, stories of consistently high quality that may sometimes make you laugh, sometimes make you cry, but are always fresh and creative and contain many delightful surprises within their pages.

Most romance fans read an enormous number of books. Those they truly love, they keep. Others may be traded with friends and soon forgotten. We hope that each LOVESWEPT romance will be a treasure—a "keeper." We will always try to publish

LOVE STORIES YOU'LL NEVER FORGET
BY AUTHORS YOU'LL ALWAYS REMEMBER

The Editors

MIDNIGHT HOUR

DEBRA DIXON

BANTAM BOOKS

NEW YORK · TORONTO · LONDON · SYDNEY · AUCKLAND

MIDNIGHT HOUR
A Bantam Book / April 1994

*If you would be interested in receiving protective vinyl covers for your
Loveswept books, please write to this address for information:*

> *Loveswept
> Bantam Books
> P.O. Box 985
> Hicksville, NY 11802*

ISBN 0-553-44430-1

Published simultaneously in the United States and Canada

To Laura Austin and Jack Berry,
not only my parents,
but also two of my very favorite people.

A special thanks to
Eric Norwood for patiently answering
questions about television,
Loretta Sheffield for shedding some light
on small emergency rooms and
Pam Ireland for knowing absolutely
everything I was going to have to fix

ONE

As soon as the little girl on his emergency-room table was out of danger, Nick Devereaux stripped off his latex gloves and allowed himself one small moment of celebration. He'd beaten death again. He smiled at the child.

"You'll be all right, *chère*," he said, his Cajun accent creeping into his speech.

His smile faded as he thought of the two hotshot paramedics who'd brought the girl in. Tonight confirmed his hunch that a pattern was forming. Those two boys kept turning up in his emergency room with patients they should have taken to another hospital. An official reprimand seemed a little too much like an arrogant power play from the new doctor in town, so Nick decided a little heart-to-heart chat was in order. As soon as possible.

Checking his watch, Nick frowned. Paramedics didn't hang around hospitals very long, especially not in the ER staff lounge at Mercy Hospital. The lounge was a spartan affair, boasting only a lumpy sofa, two chairs, a tiny refrigerator, and a primitive coffee maker. No radio. No television. Just yesterday's paper.

"I don't suppose they hung around tonight?" Nick asked the nurse who'd come in to check the IV.

"Bobby and John? They might have. They just brought in Mr. Peterson. I think he really did break his hip this time. We've got an orthopedic resident who's been working nights with him."

"Good. I'll be in the lounge having a little chat with Bobby and John."

"I'd check the waiting room first." She grinned at him. "It's after midnight on a Friday night. If they're here, they'll be clustered around the television set, trying to catch a few minutes of *The Midnight Hour* while they drink some coffee."

"Television," Nick whispered with a shake of his head. He'd moved to Louisville, Kentucky, a couple of months ago and still didn't understand the city's fascination with *The Midnight Hour*. Of course, he'd never seen the show. "Doesn't anybody in this city do anything else on Friday night except watch that show?"

The nurse laughed. "Not if they can help it." As he pushed aside the curtain to leave, she said, "Hey, Doc. You do good work."

Walking away, Nick looked over his shoulder and said, "*Oui*, but then we have no choice, you and I."

Rolling his shoulders eased the ache between them; he pushed open the door to the waiting room. He was bone-tired, only on his feet because he was too stubborn to close his eyes and too familiar with the wretched furniture that graced Mercy Hospital to sit down. He paused long enough to reassure the child's parents and tell them they could see her before the staff moved her upstairs.

The smiling couple hurried away, and Nick let his gaze sweep the depressing room. Drab green vinyl and chrome had never been favorites of his. Nor was he any fonder of gray speckled linoleum, patched so many times it resembled a crazy quilt. Institutional was the kindest adjective he could summon for the waiting room. Not warm, reassuring, or even comfortable. Just *institutional*. Considering the private, nonprofit hospital's shoestring budget, the room was never likely to become anything more.

Right now his problem wasn't the waiting room, but the two paramedics huddled in front of the old television set. They jostled one another for position and obscured the screen from Nick's view as he approached. Bobby, tall and thin, swore softly at the screen. John, who looked more like a surfer than a paramedic, intoned reverently, "Have *mercy* on my soul."

"Hold that thought," Nick advised drily. "You gonna need it by the time I'm through with you."

Both the men whirled, but John spoke first. "Hey, Doc! How's the little girl?"

Nick held on to his temper, deliberately making himself answer calmly. "She'll make it. But if you'd gone down the road ten more blocks, you could have admitted that girl to a hospital better equipped for pediatric emergencies. Gentlemen, that's the fourth patient you've delivered here who *could* have gone down the road. And I'd like to know why."

"The girl's parents asked for Mercy Hospital," John answered with a shrug. "We gotta go where the patients tell us."

"You expect me to believe that the parents wanted you to bring their child to this hospital?" Nick raised an eyebrow. "We can barely manage to scrounge up a pediatric blood-pressure cuff."

"We didn't bring her *here*," Bobby clarified with a grin. "What John's trying to say is that the parents are from the neighborhood. The word's out on the new doctor who likes working Friday-night shifts. The girl's parents figured she had a better chance with *you*. Ten blocks up the road don't have Nick Devereaux." A tone from Bobby's beeper put an end to the conversation, but as the young man backed to the door he added, "Face it, Doc, you're beginning to get a reputation around here—a reputation for getting the job done."

About to sprint away, John called over his shoulder, "You look like hell, Doc. If you won't go home, why don't you take a load off, and let Midnight Mercy do the rest?"

Nick waited until they'd gone before he dropped into the chair. He didn't need to watch television. He needed eight solid hours of sleep. Closing his eyes, Nick leaned his head back against the seat. A low sigh escaped him as he finally admitted that moving away from New Orleans hadn't changed a damn thing. He still never slept for more than four hours at a time, and he was no closer to finding a place to call home than he had been before.

Life hadn't felt right in a long time. Not since

his world fell apart years ago. Not since a voice on a telephone informed him that his parents and his little sister hadn't survived the accident.

Slowly, seductively, a woman's husky voice penetrated his thoughts of the past. It was the kind of voice that grabbed a man's soul and turned him inside out. "I'll do anything once, but even I won't invite a vampire to dinner unless he promises not to bite the neck that feeds him."

Nick's eyes flew open, and he stared at the water-stained tiles in the ceiling. Some masculine spark of self-preservation warned him to turn away from the siren's voice while he still could. Laughing at the absurdity of the thought, Nick pushed himself to a sitting position and got his first look at Mercy Malone, Louisville's hip horror queen, hostess of the Friday-night-movie showcase, *The Midnight Hour*.

"Be still my heart," Nick said aloud, and then Louisiana heat warmed his voice as he added, "*Bon Dieu, chère*, you could definitely raise the dead."

Spike heels supported legs that were probably outlawed in less progressive countries. Besides black fishnet hose, the woman wore only a tuxedo jacket, strategically buttoned somewhere in the vicinity of her waist and falling just past the sweet curve of her rump. No bra or at least not one that showed at the deep vee of the jacket.

Nick wasn't satisfied with guessing. It seemed suddenly important to know if she wore a scrap of sexy lace that pushed up the creamy flesh. Her hands slowly rubbed their way down her body, hinting at curves beneath the jacket before she tucked her red-tipped fingers into the pockets of the tux. Lost in the illusion she created, Nick leaned forward, resting his forearms on his wide-spread knees.

Russet, he decided. Her hair was russet, a deep reddish brown shot with bits of gold. Definitely long russet hair, tumbled and mussed in an incredibly sexy way. Just the way he'd muss it when he made love to her. Mercy's head was slightly tilted. One strand of hair fell artfully against her forehead and across one eye, as if begging him to reach out and push it away as he kissed her.

When the camera zoomed in for a close-up of her face, she peered up from a tangle of eyelashes and sexuality as she said, "Don't touch that . . . dial."

Nick let out a long slow breath. Mercy Malone was raising something, and he was fairly certain it wasn't the dead. No wonder the male population glued itself to the television set every Friday night. He'd heard that half the female population did too.

After seeing her, Nick understood why. Mercy might be a living, breathing male fantasy, but she didn't buy into the fantasy. The half smile and the twinkle in her eyes appealed to anyone with a sense of humor. Unfortunately, Nick was both male and possessed of a sense of humor. He didn't know whether to chuckle or take a cold shower.

During the commercial, he hauled himself out of the chair, wanting to walk off some of the energy Mercy had managed to spark within him. Calculatingly, Nick scanned the waiting room as he paced, noting again the dilapidated condition of the place. To no one in particular, he announced, "If that blue-eyed angel can raise the dead, she can probably raise a few bucks for a worthy cause." He stopped pacing. "And causes don't get more worthy than this place."

Nick nodded, satisfied with the neat solution of his two newest problems—fund-raising and Mercy Malone. Engineering a meeting might take a couple of weeks, but he never doubted for a moment that he would pull it off. As he paced he began to plan his attack. First, he needed to talk with Sister Agatha, the nun who ran Mercy Hospital. If the gossip was true, that woman had incredible connections around town. She knew virtually everybody.

Then with her approval, he'd talk to the hospital's board members. How could they say no to any scheme that would raise money for the emergency room? Rubbing his hands together, Nick realized he was finally looking forward to the future instead of getting bogged down in the past. He had places to go and people to see, all because Mercy Malone had given him an idea and jump-started his emotional battery.

Mercy stared at the disaster and thanked every one of her lucky stars that a new kitchen floor hadn't made it to the top of her remodeling list. A half hour earlier she'd climbed out of a cool shower, completely relaxed. And then disaster had struck. Or more accurately, the plumbing from hell struck and flooded her kitchen floor. Her *old* kitchen floor, she thought with some satisfaction, and reminded herself that this sort of thing was to be expected when you lived in a hundred-year-old house. In for a penny, in for a pound.

Glancing at the clock over the stove, she debated

calling the plumber's answering service again. She felt a twinge of guilt for insisting they try to track him down at his niece's dance recital, but she really hadn't had a choice. This was the only plumber in town who advertised weekend service *and* had a real live voice at the end of his telephone line. The other four numbers in the phone book were answered by a recording.

Why did disasters always happen after hours? She took some comfort from knowing that a disaster at six-thirty on a Saturday evening was probably less expensive than a Sunday-morning disaster. On second thought, any plumber pulled away from a family event was going to charge a fortune. It was either pay a fortune or stay up all night repeatedly emptying the bowl she now had under the pipe. When the doorbell sounded, Mercy smiled with relief. The cavalry had arrived! And none too soon.

On her way to the front door, she flipped tendrils of still-wet hair out of her face, grimacing slightly in the gilded entryway mirror. Maybe the plumber wasn't a fan. Otherwise he'd be disappointed to meet Mercy instead of *Midnight Mercy*.

When she opened the heavy, oak-paneled door, she wondered if this situation might not be one of Mother Nature's little practical jokes. The immaculate man in front of her had obviously come straight from the recital. While she stared at the plumber-to-die-for, she remembered she hadn't put on shoes or makeup. Her blue-jean cutoffs didn't look sexy; they looked old, and she sincerely hoped she didn't appear as scruffy as she suspected she might.

She forced a smile when she couldn't think of anything clever to say and stared. Somehow, Mercy May

Malone never managed to be quite as good at making first impressions as "Midnight Mercy Malone," who would have drawn attention to her bottom lip with a long nail and shamelessly run her eyes up and down the gorgeous masculine body on the porch. Instead, Mercy May couldn't take her gaze from *his* full sensual mouth. Or the blazing sunset that haloed him. Finally, she found her voice.

"I was just going to call your service again."

"Again?" A warm smile revealed perfect white teeth. As he smoothly pulled off a pair of wire-rim sunglasses, he uncovered almost black eyes that were every bit as expressive as his mouth, but the faint shadows beneath them made her wonder if he had gotten much sleep last night. And then she wondered what kept him up at night. He sure didn't look like any plumber she'd ever seen. This was a plumber who could make a girl jealous of her own pipes.

"I was afraid you hadn't gotten the first message," Mercy explained slowly, and resisted the urge to tug on the frayed edges of her shorts. *Oh, for God's sake, Mercy. Get a grip. He's a tired plumber, and you're a television celebrity!* Only she never felt like a celebrity unless she was dressed for the part in spike heels with fake fog swirling around her. Right now Mercy's bare feet rested flatly against the smooth surface of a newly refinished hardwood floor, and the only fog in the vicinity was swirling around her brain.

When he raised a brow and flicked his eyes pointedly at the old wood-framed screen door, Mercy instantly unlatched it and held it open, pleased it didn't squeak for once. "Oh, sorry. Come on in. You can't get anything done standing on the porch."

Without meaning to, Mercy held her breath as he stepped across her threshold, brushing so close to her that she could almost feel the heat from his body. Swallowing, Mercy decided "stepped over the threshold" was too passive a description. He didn't exactly invade her house, but he sure filled up a room. Mother Nature was indeed playing one of her little jokes—sprinkling hormones around indiscriminately.

"I'm sorry to call you away from"—Mercy gestured to his pleated, khaki slacks and starched white shirt—"your evening. I hope you have everything you need in your car. You'll probably want to change, too, after you see the mess in the kitchen. The downstairs bathroom is just past that antique telephone table."

He frowned as though he were puzzled and then said, "I've never minded a little cooking mess in the kitchen. Papa Jack said never trust a precise woman. They spend too much time measuring and not enough time enjoying. I think I agree."

His eyes gently inventoried her from top to bottom, and his voice flowed through her like hot coffee, thick with cream and sweetened just right. *Get a grip, Mercy May!* Irritated at her train of thought, she put her hands on her hips. "Cooking? Measuring? What are you talking about? I told your service everything. Didn't they give you my whole message?"

"Guess not."

"I have a leaking water pipe in my kitchen," she reminded him. At his blank look, she tried again, "Water everywhere? Frankly, I've long since run out of towels. If you don't get this fixed pronto, I'm afraid I'm going to have to donate my chenille bathrobe to the cause, Mister . . ." She paused delicately.

"Devereaux. Dr. Nick Devereaux." He spoke the words softly, intimately, like a secret shared.

"Devereaux?"

Nick listened as Mercy experimentally rolled the name off her tongue and admitted that he'd wanted to hear her say it for the last two weeks. Even if she threw him out when she realized he wasn't the plumber, at least he'd have the satisfaction of having heard his name on her lips. Perhaps if he pulled the Cajun charm out of mothballs, he wouldn't have to worry about being thrown out. Truth be told, he had no intention of being sent on his way.

Not now. Not until he got to know Mercy Malone. She surprised him, made him curious about her. He expected a celebrity and found a wonderfully real woman with a leaky pipe. He hadn't wanted to grab hold of anything in a long time. Now he did. Not her body, although God knew it was worth grabbing hold of. He wanted to hold on to the spark of interest she'd struck inside him.

"*Doctor* Devereaux?" she repeated, this time with the accent.

"N'Awlins, Lou'siana," he answered in response to her unspoken question, blending the two words of the city's name together. His accent had softened with years of practice, but he'd never managed a generic, white-bread pronunciation of either New Orleans or his name. "I'm sorry to disappoint, but if it isn't flesh and blood, I don't plumb it."

Mercy's lovely mouth dropped open and she asked, "Then *why* did they send you?"

Crossing his arms, he said, "*They* didn't send me."

"You're not the plumber?"

"No, *chère*. I'm the doctor."

"But I called for a plumber!" She rubbed her bare arms, which the shawl of damp hair had cooled. Better to believe that explanation than admit his earthy accent gave her goose bumps. "Don't tell me the service got the messages mixed up."

Nick fought a smile at the look on Mercy's face. Even disconcerted, she looked sexy. He wondered if the plumbing situation unsettled her or if the energy he felt flowing between them jumped her train off the track. Either way he enjoyed watching her massage parts of her body as she tried to figure out a solution to her predicament.

"I'm here," Nick pointed out, hoping to sidetrack her. "Maybe I could help?"

"What do you know about plumbing?"

"Only what I read in the papers," Nick answered solemnly.

"Well, that's more than me. The sum total of my knowledge is that the faucet goes on top, which is why I need a professional. No offense. Someone who can get the job done."

Nick shrugged and leaned his shoulder against the wall. "Darlin', I do have a reputation for getting the job done."

Mercy pressed her lips together. Now, why did she believe him? Clearing her throat and with a raised eyebrow, she suggested, "Let's start over, shall we? Who the heck are you?" She grinned at him as she said, "I know you're not a doctor, 'cause doctors don't make house calls anymore. Not even in a small town like Haunt, Kentucky. Especially to people who aren't patients."

Nick grinned back and decided he liked Mercy Malone as much as he was attracted to her. Wet hair, long legs, barely dressed, and a sense of humor. What more could a man ask from a celebrity fund-raiser? Or a woman for that matter, Nick added, surprising himself as he realized that Mercy's most attractive quality was her sense of humor. That's why he instinctively responded to her. Listening to her made him feel good.

"I really am a doctor," Nick said, and pushed away from the wall. "I recently joined the emergency-room staff at a hospital in Louisville."

"Things must be slow if you're roaming the countryside in search of emergencies," she quipped.

Nick ignored the remark and dropped the other shoe. "You probably know the hospital. Mercy Hospital? I understand you were born there."

Startled, she almost backed through the screen door. "How do you know that?"

"Sister Agatha still runs the hospital. She remembers you and your parents quite well. Even tracked down your address for me. Told me that when I saw you, I was to request—strongly—that you get your butt over for a visit."

"Sister Aggie?" Mercy smiled, using the childhood name she'd called the nun. She lowered her head in contemplation, fondly remembering the no-nonsense woman. "I haven't seen her since I was nineteen and having impure thoughts about one of the residents." Suddenly Mercy's head jerked up, and she took a couple of steps toward him. "Has she seen the show?"

Nick nodded once, but didn't volunteer a word.

"What did she say?"

With a straight face, Nick tactfully edited Sister Agatha's comment and merely said, "She thought perhaps now that your show is a success you could afford to buy more material for your costumes."

Laughing, Mercy said, "Sister Aggie has either mellowed or you're trying to spare my feelings. Which is it?"

Nick shifted uncomfortably and rubbed his chin. "Mellow is not exactly the word I'd use to describe Sister Agatha."

"Not *exactly* the word? Why do I get the feeling you've given a lot of thought to the matter of describing her in one word?"

"It's a habit of mine."

Mercy put her hands on her hips and studied him for a minute. "What's the definitive word for Sister Aggie?"

"Perceptive."

"Agreed. What did she say about my show?"

"She said she was praying that you'd find a husband soon so you could stop advertising."

"She said *what*!" Mercy's body went rigid, her hands falling to her sides in small white-knuckled fists.

"She said—" Nick began helpfully.

"I know what she said!" Mercy eyed him suspiciously, opening and closing her hands in an obvious attempt to control her temper. "What the hell are you supposed to be? The answer to her prayers?"

"Actually, darlin', I was kind of hoping you were the answer to mine." Nick recognized the real truth in that statement.

"Of course." Mercy nodded and stepped closer,

folding her arms across her midriff. She checked for a wedding ring. He wasn't wearing one, which led her to an interesting conclusion: Sister Agatha was matchmaking. "Dr. Devereaux, you are one smooth son of a gun, but you go right back and tell Sister Aggie I'm a damn sight smarter now than I was at nineteen. I can spot a heartbreaker fifty yards away."

"Ah no, I'm a doctor, *chère*," Nick argued gently, remembering Sister Agatha's insistence that he make the trip instead of phoning. "I don't break hearts. I mend 'em."

"But my heart doesn't need mending. By you or anyone else," she told him with a toss of her head, giving him a taste of the provocative Midnight Mercy. "Sister Agatha should realize that. Don't you two ever watch television? Mercy Malone is in the business of breaking hearts, not the other way round."

"Now, *that* I believe, but it doesn't scare me off."

"My breaking your heart doesn't scare you?"

"No, being the first man to break yours doesn't scare me," he deadpanned. For a second he saw surprise flare in her eyes and knew, however unintentionally, he'd scored a direct hit. Mercy Malone was off balance, and she wasn't used to being off balance. Nick decided he liked her that way.

Mercy felt as though the gauntlet had just been flung, that her honor was at stake. She wanted to wipe that smug, sexy, irritating smile off the doctor's face. *Doctor!* That certainly explained a lot about his attitude. She had grown up with surgeons for parents and knew exactly how futile it was to argue with doctors who thought they were right. But that never stopped her from trying.

"I'm twenty-nine years old, Dr. Devereaux. Trust me," she said in a confidential tone. "I've had plenty of opportunities for broken hearts."

"Aw, darlin'," Nick said with a shake of his head. "But how many of those . . . opportunities did you take advantage of?"

Irrationally, Mercy wanted Devereaux to leave so she wouldn't have to answer the incriminating question, and she wanted him to stay until she found out exactly what Sister Agatha had told him! Never before had anyone questioned Midnight Mercy's experience, even in jest. Usually people tended to mix up her television persona with her private self. As she studied him Mercy drew attention to her bottom lip with one long red fingernail.

"You're *so* sure that I've never suffered a broken heart," she mused, infusing her voice with the same teasing sexuality she used on television. "Is that a professional diagnosis, Doctor?"

"Oh no. I haven't asked the question."

"What question?"

"A simple one. Who broke your heart?"

Nonplussed, Mercy floundered for a snappy reply, and then just tried to figure out something he'd believe.

As the silence stretched, Nick briefly considered letting the subject drop, but only briefly. The sexy, confident Mercy Malone he'd seen on television seemed perfectly capable of telling him to go to hell, and she hadn't. So he didn't back off. "What'sa matter, *chère*? Don't remember the details?"

"I'm thinking."

"You're stalling," he corrected, and turned away

from her, walking toward the wide carpeted stairway that led to the second story. "I'd think twice about getting a dog if I were you. This newel post looks like a giant, hand-carved fireplug."

Exasperated, Mercy gave a small huff, and not just because he'd insulted her post. "How am I supposed to think with you talking all the time?"

"You shouldn't have to think. Any woman who's had her heart broken knows every little detail. She knows who, and where, and when. The lady can even tell you the moment it happened. But not you." Nick ran his hand along the highly polished banister. He missed her widened eyes, and the way she followed the motion of his hand. Nick paused for a heartbeat and then added, "Now, why is that?"

The sharp ring of the telephone caught them both by surprise, breaking the spell of intimacy that had been weaving itself around the two of them. When Mercy didn't move, Nick said, "I believe someone is callin' you."

"I can hear," she replied, and walked past him to the phone table. Snatching up the black bone-shaped receiver, she answered more sharply than she intended and silently swore she'd wipe that self-satisfied look off Devereaux's face if it was the last thing she did on this earth. "Oh . . . Sophie, hi. No, nothing's wrong."

Nick chuckled and wandered toward the opening into the living room, which looked comfortable but still reflected the century-old character of the house. Without sacrificing any of the architectural flavor, Mercy had managed to make an inviting home—something he hadn't been able to do with his apartment even though he'd hired an interior-design firm.

"No, he's not the plumber," Mercy patiently explained to her elderly neighbor as she eyed her guest. "He's a doctor. No, I'm not sick. Devereaux. Dr. Devereaux. No, not France. He's from New Orleans. Yes, the one in Louisiana."

When he heard his name, eavesdropping became too great a temptation for Nick, but he salved his conscience by facing her so she'd know he was shamelessly snooping. Fleetingly, Nick wondered if she'd forgotten her plumbing problems as completely as he'd forgotten about being tired.

"No!" Mercy's answer to the unheard question was sharp. Suddenly she clenched her teeth as though trying to hold out against pressure. She shot him a furtive glance, then turned away and lowered her voice. "No, I'm fine. Really. Now is not a good time, Sophie. Sophie . . . Sophie!"

Gingerly, Mercy replaced the receiver. She turned and announced, "We're about to have company. Sophie would like to meet you. She's never met anyone from New Orleans."

Something in Mercy's tone of voice straightened Nick's spine. He ran his fingers through his hair. "Should I be worried?"

Mercy's sense of humor began to surface and her mouth twitched. "I would. She's afraid you're ravishing me."

"She's afraid I'm *what*?"

"Ravishing me," Mercy said pleasantly as she passed him on her way to the screen door to wait for Sophie.

"You can't be serious," Nick declared.

"Oh, I'm perfectly serious. Sophie says she saw

you drive up and you're just the sort of man who might, and I quote, *try something*."

"And Midnight Mercy is just the sort of woman who could handle it if I did," Nick replied sharply.

A shiver raced up her spine. He had used her nickname. "Why did you call me that? I mean— Midnight Mercy. Why'd you call me that?"

"*Chère*, I look at you and see two incredibly sexy women who excite the hell out of this poor Cajun." He joined her by the door and leaned against the jamb. Mercy Malone was a complicated woman; not what he had expected, and she fascinated him. He gently lifted her chin and forced her to look at him as he explained. "One woman breaks hearts so easily while the other seems to be very careful with her own."

This time the shiver raced through her entire body, and a flush of heat quickly followed. The new intensity in his eyes belied the shadows beneath them. Nick no longer looked like he needed sleep; he looked dangerously intent on getting what he wanted.

"Mercy dear!" Sophie called out as she started up the porch steps. As usual in the summer, Mercy's neighbor wore a comfortable and brightly embroidered Mexican sundress. "I just needed to borrow a little brown sugar. You don't mind, do you?" Sophie crossed the wooden porch and affected surprise, "Oh, dear me! I see you're busy at the moment."

Startled, Mercy realized that Nick's thumb was slowly but surely tracing her collarbone as he slid her soft, white cotton shirt off the shoulder. "Oh, for God's sake," Mercy ground out, and shrugged off Nick's hand. "Come on in, Sophie."

This time when she opened the screen door, it screeched its usual banshee protest. Once the sprightly octogenarian scooted inside, Mercy made the introductions. "Sophie Jensen, Dr. Nick Devereaux. There. All introduced."

Without rushing, Sophie tapped the plastic measuring cup against her thigh, sized Nick up, and said, "So how long have you known our Mercy?"

Nick laughed, crossed his arms, and gave her an equally careful once-over. "Not quite long enough to ravish her, but don't you worry. I'm wearing her down."

Mercy choked and muttered hopelessly, "Oh God, what else can happen today?"

"My!" Sophie exclaimed as though nothing embarrassing had transpired. "Don't the floors look nice. This entrance hall seems enormous now that you've gotten all that nasty old green carpeting out of here. Mary Jane Hiller, rest her soul, did so like shag carpeting. But this is much better, dear. More spacious."

"You think so?" Mercy took the cup from Sophie and looked pointedly at the two of them. "I was just thinking how crowded it felt. You two get acquainted while I swim through the kitchen and get some sugar."

"Oh dear, your plumbing problem!" Sophie snatched her cup back from Mercy's hand. "I wouldn't think of borrowing sugar at a time like this. I'll just run down the street to Joan's and get some sugar there." She whisked the door open before Mercy could protest. "Nice to have met you, Doctor."

"A pleasure to be met, I assure you," Nick said,

and reached to flip on the porch light. "It's beginning to get dark. I wouldn't want you to slip before you got that sugar."

"How thoughtful," Sophie murmured as she toddled off. "Now, Mercy," she said, "you call me if you need me."

Mercy shook her head. "What I need is a plumber."

"I offered to help," Nick reminded her.

Without taking her gaze from the receding figure of Sophie, Mercy asked, "And which of us do you want to help? Midnight Mercy or Mercy May Malone?"

TWO

"Now why do I feel like I just entered the bonus round of Truth or Dare?" Nick asked, and walked away, shaking his head. "Not being stupid, I think I'll let that sleepin' dog lie a bit longer. Which way to the kitchen?"

Mercy shut the wooden door and leaned against it. To his back she primly said, "I haven't said you could help."

Nick chuckled and kept walking toward the rear of the house. "You haven't told me to leave either. Besides"—he paused and opened a door, finding the downstairs bathroom mentioned earlier—"if I left now, you'd have Sophie over here in five minutes wanting to know why you ran off such a promising young man." He flashed her a confident grin. "Careful. I think that one kinda likes me, *chère*."

Following him, Mercy grumbled, "She can afford to be generous with her opinion. Sophie has lower standards and sounder plumbing than I do."

"Ah, getting warmer," Nick announced, and stepped into the dining room, glancing first at the elegant cherry table and sideboard. Then he noticed the eight mismatched chairs. As he passed through on his way to what he assumed would be the kitchen, he discovered that not only was every chair of a completely different style, but the needlepoint seats were mismatched as well. "What you runnin' here, darlin'? A home for orphan chairs? Nice rug, though. Persian?"

"Chinese silk," she snapped. "And don't talk like that about my chairs. I'll have you know that each and every one of these babies probably has a better pedigree than you."

Nick pivoted and bumped the swinging door open with his backside while he made a point. "Well now, maybe they do, but I can keep you warm all night, and that makes me the better bargain, no?"

Only the fact that he disappeared into the kitchen stopped Mercy from informing him that she had a perfectly adequate electric blanket upstairs. Of course, he would have had something to say about that too. Something devastating like "Ah, chère," which he'd say with a sad shake of his head, as though having to use an electric blanket was a poor substitute for having a man in her bed. A man like Nick Devereaux to be exact. Unfortunately, Mercy was beginning to agree with him.

"Get a grip," she whispered to herself. She wasn't in the market for a man, didn't need her hormones all screwed up. Besides, her bed was warm enough without Nick Devereaux's hot body sliding between the sheets. There she went again! What on earth was it about this take-charge Cajun that had her mind constantly on the bedroom?

The man was too damn clever for his own good. Too damn sexy for her peace of mind. She stared at the kitchen door and knew that if she had an ounce of common sense, she'd march right back to the phone and try to get a real plumber over here fast. Someone with grungy overalls and a fully loaded tool belt. Someone named Ralph. Someone who didn't have dark, smoldering eyes and thick black hair begging for her fingers.

However, pride kept her from making the call. Good ol' St. Nick wouldn't have been offended by her lack of confidence in his plumbing skills. Oh no, not him. He'd interpret a call to the real plumber as a cowardly way to get rid of him. And he'd be right, her conscience added. Face it. The man had her pegged. She was beginning to wonder if he didn't have some voodoo magic charm in his pocket.

How else could he know that she *never* encouraged relationships? What was the point of encouraging them anyway? Judging from the marriages of her friends and their parents, and her own parents, the vows should be changed from "until death us do part" to "until we get a better offer." Nope, relationships that began brilliantly and ended bitterly were not her style. She liked her heart in one piece, thank you very much.

The men who'd come her way over the last few years had been either intimidated by Midnight Mercy, satisfied just to be seen in public with her, or civilized enough to take a simple hint that she wasn't interested. Unfortunately, she doubted much of anything intimidated Nick or that he'd be satisfied by anything that could be done in public. Heck, she wasn't completely sure he was civilized. Which meant that hints wouldn't work on the man either. That much was obvious, if the noises in her kitchen could be believed. She hadn't known Nick Devereaux an hour yet, and he was poking around under her sink, making himself right at home.

Steeling herself for another round with the Bayou Bomber, Mercy entered her kitchen warily and told herself that Nick and Sister Agatha probably had something more than matchmaking in mind, or he wouldn't have driven an hour to see her. All his charm and the Mr. Helpful routine were most likely part of his plan to soften her up. She sighed, knowing the plan was working.

Just as she'd left them earlier, all the cleaning supplies normally stored under the cabinet covered the top of the oak table by the picture window, and the huge, orange plastic bowl was still under the pipe. Nick was hunkered down in front of the open cabinet, shining a flashlight in a thoroughly competent way. Unhappily, she acknowledged the fact that Mr. Helpful looked pretty good to her right now.

"The first thing we gotta do is shut off the water," he told her as he inched closer, reaching inside to run his hand over an old copper pipe.

"But I already did that," she told him. "I shut off those valves under there before I called the plumber. Obviously, they don't work."

"For this, they aren't supposed to. Your leaky pipe is a supply line." He waved her over, pointing at the two valves separating the incoming pipes from the copper tubing leading to the fixtures. "When you turned those, all you did was cut off the supply to the faucet. Water still comes right up to the valves from the main line. First, we shut off the water at the street. Then we fix your pipe."

"We can do that? You really know what you're doing?" Mercy asked, amazed that Nick hadn't been overwhelmed at the thought of wielding a wrench. Her father always had been. His motto had been that doctors, by reason of higher education, were above manual labor. Pretty funny considering both her parents were surgeons and, technically, performed manual labor all day.

Flicking off the flashlight, Nick looked up and enjoyed the view of long shapely thighs disappearing into a fringe of frayed denim. "Give me a little time, *chère*. I'll get the job done. All I need is the key."

Mercy straightened and scooted away, aware that his voice made promises that had nothing to do with her plumbing. Nervously, she brushed her long hair back from her face with her fingers and fought back another urge to tug on her shorts. Instead, she cleared her throat and tucked her hands in her back pockets, coincidentally shoving the material down to cover more of her thighs. "I don't think I have one. When I bought this place, all they gave me was the house key."

"Not that kind of key," Nick explained as he stood up and placed the light carefully on the spotless counter. *Mon Dieu*, Mercy jumped like he was a 'gator trying to snap a bite out of her. Nick reined in his disappointed libido and turned his attention to the plumbing problem. "The key we need is a long, heavy, metal gadget that looks like the letter *T*. You got one of those around here?"

With a short laugh, Mercy rolled her eyes and held up fingers as she counted off her meager tool supply. "I've got a hammer, a screwdriver, a wrench, some sandpaper, which has seen better days, and a big yellow book full of phone numbers for electricians, painters, plumbers, and roofers. Get the picture?"

Scanning the outdated kitchen with its limited counter space like a contractor calculating profit, Nick said, "You're gonna need more reliable phone numbers or some better tools if you plan to drag this kitchen into the twentieth century."

"Who the hell are you?" Mercy asked with some irritation. "A spy for *Better Homes and Gardens*? You've insulted my newel post, my chairs, and now my kitchen. Why on earth did you come here?"

Nick rubbed the back of his neck and considered how best to answer the question. If Sister Agatha was right, the minute Mercy heard about the hospital's need for a better emergency room, she'd jump at the chance to help and send him off with a promise to have her people call him. In the last half hour Nick had become interested in more than Mercy's help with fund-raising, and he sure as hell didn't want to spend his time talking to her people. If he'd wanted to do that, he would have tried a little harder over the last couple of weeks to convince that grizzly bear of a station manager to give him an appointment.

"I don't suppose you'd believe I'm a devoted fan?" he asked.

"Not on a bet." Mercy folded her arms and waited patiently. She almost tapped her foot against the black-and-white vinyl floor, then wisely decided not to draw any more attention to her bare legs. "Dr. Devereaux, you may not think I'm an expert on broken hearts, but I do know fans. They gush, get terribly shy, find something for me to sign, or act too sophisticated for autographs. But you know what?" Mercy shifted her hands to her hips. "They hardly ever insult me."

A slow smile worked its way onto Nick's face as he dug in his pocket for a piece of paper. He found a gas credit-card receipt, which he held out. "May I have your autograph, Miss Malone?"

"Too little, too late," Mercy informed him, but a smile tugged at the corner of her mouth. Subduing it, she said, "If you're a fan, then I'm Tinkerbell. Since I don't have wings, you must not be a fan. Now, exactly what is it that you and Sister want from me, Dr. Devereaux?"

"To begin, you could call me Nick." He shoved the receipt back into his pocket. "And I am most definitely a fan. Devoted in fact. I never, ever, touch the dial."

"What do you want, *Nick*."

"A small favor."

"Ah, I see. This is the part where you tell me that you'll fix my plumbing if I do you a little favor." Although she'd guessed as much, Mercy was still disappointed that Nick Devereaux had taken advantage of her situation. It was such a . . . a . . . typically *macho* scheme, and she'd begun to hope that Nick wasn't typical at all.

He slanted a glance at her and shook his head. "No, darlin'. This is the part where I ask you if you could finish grilling me on the way to the hardware store. That is, assuming you have one in this town, and it's still open."

"Of course we have a hardware store. Haunt, Kentucky, isn't exactly a big city, but it's not the back end of nowhere either. We hardly ever roll up the sidewalks at six o'clock."

"Then find some shoes, Mercy Malone." He dusted off his hands. "We need to visit the hardware man and find out if he has a shutoff key and a half-inch pipe sleeve."

"Only if I drive," she said quickly, as if being the driver magically gave her control of the situation. Not that it truly mattered. Right now she'd consider dancing with the devil if he'd fix her pipe. In comparison, a little car ride with Nick didn't seem so bad.

"Of course you'll drive," Nick agreed smoothly. When she was halfway through the door, he added, "I figured that out from the get-go. I'm just coming along for the ride."

Mercy stopped dead in her tracks, but didn't turn around. All she'd find was an innocent expression and smoldering eyes, and she refused to give him the satisfaction.

Conversation on the way to and returning from the hardware store had been harmless enough, Mercy decided. They talked about the weather—unusually warm for the end of May; horse racing—they were both fans of the racetrack; cuisine—Nick chided her for never having eaten crawfish étouffée even though she'd been to New Orleans a number of times; and cars—Nick's restored '67 Chevelle hot rod versus the classy styling of Mercy's old Jaguar, both black and both beloved. They talked about anything and everything except why Nick had driven down to Haunt, Kentucky.

The longer the good doctor avoided the subject of his "little favor," the more intrigued Mercy became. Now as she followed him through the house and into the kitchen again, she had to admit that he wasn't typical at all. He fully intended to fix her pipe whether or not she agreed to do his favor.

Nick tossed the sack of plumbing parts on the counter and handed her the tool they had used to shut off the water. "Judging from the age of this house and the state of your plumbing, you'd better put this someplace handy. You'll be needing it."

"Thank you," Mercy said as graciously as possible. "At least I'll know how to use it *if* I do need it again."

A deep, low chuckle accompanied Nick's warning. "Oh, you gonna need it again."

"Careful," Mercy said pleasantly. "You're insulting a woman with a heavy metal object in her hands."

Nick waved off the danger and rummaged through the paper bag, grabbing the pipe sleeve. "I'm safe. I haven't fixed your pipe yet. Afterward I'll watch my mouth." Mischief lit his eyes as he quickly looked at her. "I might even watch your mouth if you sweet-talk me."

"I've never been much good at sweet talking," Mercy said, and silently wished she were. With a clever script and in front of a camera, she could sweet-talk the best of them, but not in real life. Not in her kitchen staring at a man who knew the difference between

Mercy May and Midnight Mercy. He panicked even the butterflies in her stomach.

"Ah, talking sweet is easy," he promised, leaning toward her. "All you gonna need is a willing victim and a little practice."

Mercy swallowed and tried to ignore the heat rising in her checks. She knew that to sensual men like Nick, the chase was as instinctive as drawing breath, but the knowledge didn't stop the flutter of anticipation or the feeling that she was special. Flirting with the doctor was a bit like playing with fireworks—lighting the fuse guaranteed an explosion. He created an unfamiliar sensation in her: he made her feel like Midnight Mercy, capable of holding her own with a dangerous man. Holding her own and more.

Uncharacteristically, Mercy struck a match and lit the fuse. In a sultry voice, she asked, "And I suppose you're the willing victim?"

Very slowly and with a lingering glance on her mouth, Nick volunteered, "Absolutely ready, completely willing, and more than able."

The air in the room vanished, leaving Mercy struggling to pull enough oxygen into her lungs. She understood the implied invitation to put him to the test. Silence hung in the air while she debated whether or not to RSVP. Although she still clutched the large metal key to her chest like a shield, she finally swayed toward him just as he winked and backed off.

"But first, I've gotta fix this damn pipe." Nick turned away and carefully studied the undersink area, giving her time to get a grip on herself. He tugged on his trouser legs and crouched in front of the opening. Pulling away hadn't been easy. If she'd been the woman he'd expected when he rang the doorbell, he wouldn't have pulled away. He'd have kissed her and let nature take its course.

Unfortunately, Mercy Malone was more and less than the heart-stopping woman on *The Midnight Hour*. His dandy little plan to mix business and pleasure had hit a snag—his conscience. Cursing the sudden appearance of the principles his parents had drummed into him, Nick said, "If you can get me an old shirt and a hair dryer, I'll start."

"A hair dryer? What kind of shirt?" Mercy asked, slightly dazed from having her lit fuse abruptly snuffed out. Her brain tried to work out why he needed a shirt and a hair dryer, as well as why she remained unkissed when she had been so certain she was about to be kissed!

"A big shirt. Something that'll go over these shoulders," he explained as he reached over to grab the dishtowel draped through the refrigerator handle. Carefully, he wiped down the pipe, which no longer trickled water into the orange bowl. "The cleaners have a hell of a time getting those green corrosion stains out of white dress shirts."

As the silence grew he twisted around. "I'm not picky. Anything will do. An old jersey left by a beau, a flannel shirt—"

At her frown, Nick caught on. Mercy didn't have any clothing trophies from the past, because she didn't let men into her life. At least, not intimately enough to leave spare clothing. Instincts he relied on every day in the emergency room assured him of that.

Nick stood up and crossed the room. "What'sa matter, *chère?*"

"I don't have any," she confessed, and put the key down.

"Beaux or shirts?" The question was pushing his luck, and Nick knew it. So he wasn't surprised at her frown. He didn't expect Mercy to take the bait; he wouldn't drag her into another discussion about her past this soon or this easily. Not as long as Mercy clearly wanted to avoid conversation about her history with men or lack thereof.

Her lack thereof bothered Nick more than he wanted to admit. Midnight Mercy had been fair game, but the woman in front of him was a different bowl of gumbo entirely. Judging from her response to every sexual innuendo he made, she knew how the game was played, but Nick was beginning to wonder how many she'd actually finished.

Mercy ignored the soft spoken question about her love life and pointed toward the sink. As sweetly as she could, she suggested, "Why don't you show me what to do? I'll do it, and you won't have to worry about the cleaners."

"No problem," Nick assured her. "I'll improvise." Without rushing or taking his eyes off Mercy's face, he began to unbutton his shirt. By the time he'd undone the cuffs and four buttons, Mercy visibly gulped. Her mouth opened and closed on an unspoken comment.

"I'll get the hair dryer," she finally blurted, and beat a hasty retreat.

When she left, Nick shook his head. "Ah, *chère*. How we gonna get anywhere if you keep running away?"

He tugged the shirt out of his pants, stripped it off, and draped it over a kitchen chair in one quick motion. Smiling, he noticed that all four kitchen chairs were also unique in design. Didn't the woman believe in buying sets of anything? Did she really like the eclectic look or was she simply a sucker for strays?

Isn't that what you hope, Nick? That Mercy's a sucker for strays? Strays like Nick Devereaux? That she'll add you to her collection before you even have time to blink, and then you finally can stop feeling so goddamn lonely?

Frowning, Nick felt his jaw tighten and forced himself to relax. Where in hell had those thoughts come from? He was as tired of having this argument with himself as he was tired of counting the revolutions of the ceiling fan at two in the morning. He didn't need someone in his life. Being alone and being lonely were two separate issues. The first did not necessarily cause the second.

Before he could settle the old argument, Mercy returned with the hair dryer, hesitating for a split second as she took in the sight of the half-naked doctor. She recovered nicely and pasted a smile on her face as she handed him the dryer. "I will admit to curiosity. What are you going to do with this?"

"Something kinky, of course." He laughed at the expression on her face. "No, *chère*, I just want the pipe completely dry before I put the sleeve on," Nick explained, plugging in the dryer. "And this will save me some time."

While Nick worked, Mercy stood out of the way, quietly enjoying the play of light against his well-defined muscles as he flexed, stretched, and twisted his body. Even the dreary subject of plumbing repairs as he told her what he was doing and why didn't rob his voice of that earthy, seductive resonance. Too bad she didn't want a man cluttering up her life. Nick almost made her wish she did. In fact, Sister Agatha had probably been counting on Nick's appeal.

"Done," Nick pronounced as he tightened the cylindrical rubber-and-metal clamp that securely gloved the faulty section of pipe. Standing up and tossing the towel onto the counter with a flourish, he leaned against the edge, arms folded. He grinned at her, obviously waiting for applause.

"I am suitably impressed," she said simply, keeping her eyes above his collarbone despite the urge for a closer look at the small gold medallion he wore. "Thanks, Nick. I really do appreciate your help."

"That wasn't a standing ovation, but it was sincere. So, you're welcome." As he ran his fingers through his hair he offered a little advice, "If I were you, I'd order that set of home-repair books advertised on television."

"My house is not that bad!" Mercy retorted. Giving him a sour look, she gathered up the empty sack and crumpled it into a tight ball. "This is a great house, a house with character and charm."

"This *great* house is like a great car with ninety thousand miles on the odometer and no warranty. Trust me, Mercy. The fun has just begun. You can count on it. Take it from a man who restored a twenty-five-year-old car with a great deal more than ninety thousand miles of wear and tear."

The wall phone by the backdoor rang in Mercy's ear before she could argue. She held up an index finger, the international symbol that said "Stop: We're not through yet."

"Hello. Joan?" Mercy's shoulders slumped and she sighed. "Sophie told you about my plumbing problem? No, the plumber never came. Never called. The car? It belongs to a . . . friend of mine who's helping with the pipe. What friend?"

Nick shrugged into his shirt and grinned. He remembered small-town grapevines. Louisiana had its share of concerned neighbors. He pointed at the key on the table and then outside to let her know he was about to turn the water back on.

"His name is Nick Devereaux. Not long." As he left, Mercy stared at a spot between his shoulder blades and lied, "Perfectly safe, Joan. He's harmless."

This time it was Nick's turn to pause in the doorway for a half second. Mercy grinned to herself as he kept walking. While supplying yes-and-no answers whenever Joan paused for breath, Mercy untangled the long cord and walked across to the sink. "Hmm . . . No . . . Yes, of course . . . Did she? . . . You're the chairman?"

When she judged Nick had had time to accomplish his mission, she turned on the faucet slightly, mixing cold and hot water evenly. Anyone looking at her would have thought a minor miracle occurred when the water poured through the faucet and none leaked through the patch. "It worked! . . . Oh, no. Not you, Joan. I was talking to myself."

Nick walked in and Mercy beamed, pointing at the sink and getting out of his way so he could check the miracle for himself.

"No, Joan, I won't forget. You know me, I'm a sucker for a good cause. If you think someone's going to bid fifty dollars for a Mercy Malone picnic basket, then I'll be glad to contribute a basket. Look, Joan, I have company. Could I call you back about this? . . . Thanks."

Very pleased with himself, Nick closed the cabinet doors and turned off the faucet. When he heard the click of the phone returning to the wall, he said, "Darlin', I believe you owe me dinner."

Since he'd saved her a night of worrying and a hefty service charge, Mercy had to agree. She picked up the phone again, punched in a number, and looked at Nick. "With or without anchovies?"

Nick sat at the oak table, chair pushed back and a half-empty imported beer bottle cradled on his thigh as he considered his chances of survival if he reached for the last piece of pizza. Slim at best, he decided, so he gallantly offered what he knew better than to take in the first place. "Go ahead, Mercy. You tackle that last piece before my conscience starts laying on the guilt trip about starving children of the Third World."

"Ha! You're just afraid I might stab you if you try and take it," she teased, well aware of her lumberjack appetite.

A wide grin answered her. "Well now, the possibility of your stabbing me with that knife did cross my mind."

"Okay, so now you know the real reason I moved to Haunt. Tony's Pizza-To-Go is to die for. 'Almost Heaven' is his trademark pizza and worth every extra lap I'll have to swim at the pool tomorrow."

Nick watched as she shook more of the dried hot pepper topping onto the piece. Hot and spicy.

How he normally preferred his women. Until he met Mercy and discovered he liked sexy and wholesome just as much as hot and spicy. At this moment Mercy was the farthest thing from an enchantress that Nick would have found, but nevertheless, he was completely spellbound.

Except for the tiny smudge of pizza sauce on her cheek, her complexion was flawless. Untamed russet hair fell several inches past her shoulders in shiny waves. Clear blue eyes twinkled at him as she bit the point off the last slice of pizza.

Taking a pull on his beer, Nick contemplated how content he felt here. He couldn't remember the last time he sat in a kitchen, backdoor open, listening to the patter of soft summer rain against the porch. Another pull on the beer, and a memory surfaced all too clearly. Not since Bayou Teche. *Maman* always said he was happiest with rain on the roof. Seemed the only nights he slept anymore were wet nights when the steady thrum of rain lulled him to sleep.

Only a fool would have missed the world-weary shadow in Nick's eyes as he rubbed his thumb across the label of his beer bottle. Mercy didn't miss it, noting that Nick looked sad as well as tired. She tossed the crust back into the carton and asked, "Are you ever going to tell me why you drove all the way out here?"

"Does that mean I've aroused your interest?"

"Piqued my curiosity," Mercy rephrased instantly.

She scooped up the pizza box and deposited it in the kitchen garbage, which was a heavyweight durable plastic container suitable for curbside pickup, then secured the lid tightly with an elastic cord that spanned the top of the lid, and hooked under the rim of each side.

"Expecting raccoons to invade the house tonight?" asked Nick, amused by her complicated routine.

"No, my dog does a fine job all by herself."

Startled, Nick looked quickly around. "I missed an entire dog?"

Mercy laughed and started toward the front of the house, waving for him to follow. "She's gone right now. She's in Memphis with the stud of her dreams. The breeder wanted a litter out of her, and I promised when I bought her that I'd breed her one time when she finished her championship. I miss her, but she'll be back next week after she's been bred."

In the living room, Nick immediately chose her favorite wingback chair, which was set at an angle to the sofa. When he sat down he propped his feet up on the matching midnight-blue ottoman and nodded his approval at her. The ease with which he made himself at home in her house was not lost on Mercy.

Opting for the navy-and-cream striped sofa, Mercy said, "My life is going to go to the dogs in about nine weeks. That's when the puppies will be due, assuming everything works out the way Mother Nature intended."

"One way or another everything always works out exactly the way Mother Nature intends." Nick nestled his head against the right angle of the wingback and enjoyed the view of Mercy's legs. "Try and cross Mother Nature, and the old broad will make your life a living hell. So what kind of dog do you have? Considering that you live in a town named Haunt, I assume it's something suitably spooky like a hound of Baskerville?"

"Nothing so dramatic, I'm afraid, but still appropriate for Haunt—a black Labrador retriever named Witch."

"Clever name."

"I thought so."

Companionable silence stretched between them as Nick lounged in the big chair. Finally Mercy prompted, "The favor?"

"Right, the favor. Mercy Hospital is a small hospital with an even smaller budget in an economically disadvantaged neighborhood."

Mercy nodded. "This I know."

"Sister Agatha's order has run that place for forty years, and done a fine job for the most part. Now, she would be the first to admit that the extraordinary load of charity cases drains hospital resources, but she also adamantly refuses to bring in administration specialists. Bean counters like that would crunch the numbers and increase profitability by reducing services and charity beds."

"And Sister Agatha won't let that happen."

Nick adjusted a little for comfort. "All of which means that basic simple health care and not cutting-edge medicine is practiced at Mercy Hospital."

"This I also know," she repeated. "You certainly take your time getting to the point."

"I've never had any complaints, *chère*."

He didn't move a muscle, but Mercy felt the intensity of his response like a wave of flame. God! Was there anything the man couldn't turn into sexual innuendo? "What do you want, a donation? You want me to put the financial bite on my parents, who got their start at Mercy Hospital? What?"

Ignoring her impatience, Nick continued in the same calm, reasonable voice in which he'd begun, "We're seeing big increases in elderly and disabled patients who can't afford health insurance or early treatment, which means they put off getting help until it's critical. Most of our patients come from the area around the hospital, which isn't the wealthiest or safest of neighborhoods."

Mercy made an abrupt derisive noise. "Well now, there's a news flash, Slick. Can I just say yes and get this community history over with? Whatever it is you want, I'm sure it's a wonderful idea and a worthy cause. I'll write a check. You don't have to sell me!"

"I'll take the check, but that's not what I want. No, I am afraid I need more than that. I want you."

THREE

The silence was so complete, Nick thought perhaps even the grandfather clock in the hallway had stopped ticking. Bit by bit, the world began to breathe again; the rain pattered ceaselessly again; and the clock began to tock. Nick allowed himself to relax even more in the accommodating chair and gave his body up to the familiar tiredness that haunted him. Otherwise he might have had the energy to smile at Mercy's widened eyes.

"Excuse me?" she said softly, almost in a whisper.

"I thought I made myself perfectly clear. I want you, Mercy Malone," Nick repeated lazily.

"I know what you said. I want to know what you meant!"

"I want your help with a fund-raiser. What'd you think I meant?"

The color flaming in her cheeks made it clear exactly what she thought. Nick made a disappointed clucking sound. "It is hard to have a conversation with you, darlin', when your mind is constantly on sex. Is there a particular reason you associate everything I say with lovemaking?"

Mercy narrowed her eyes and stood up. "Tell Sister I'll call a few people and see what kind of money I can drum up."

"Yeah, well, this is the tricky part." Nick adjusted his head to look up at her, but he didn't stand. He wasn't sure he could wake his muscles long enough to heave himself out of the chair.

"The calls would be nice," he agreed, "but what I need is a splashy *event*. I'm not looking to raise a few picayune thousand. No, *chère*, the hospital needs to revamp the emergency unit from the bottom up. For that, I'm gonna need Midnight Mercy in all her glory. I'm gonna need you to whip Louisville into a fever pitch, and when you do . . . I want a thousand of them to fork over one hundred dollars a plate for an evening with you and a chance to host *The Midnight Hour*."

Slowly, Mercy eased back down on the sofa, partly because she sensed that this was important to Nick—despite his casual air—and partly because of the exhaustion she saw creeping into his expression. "That's some evening you're planning, Nick. Why didn't you call the station? They take care of the promotional end. They love good deeds that generate publicity."

"Now, there's a clever idea." Nick rubbed his eyes with a thumb and index finger as though he couldn't believe he had to spell it out. "I've been trying to convince your station manager for two weeks. To do this thing right, I want the television station to kick in airtime and produce the promos, not to mention letting somebody host your show."

"Dan didn't say anything to me about it." Mercy frowned, leaned back into the striped pillows, and propped her feet on the edge of the coffee table. "He usually checks with me before turning down a charity request for my help. It's sort of an unspoken agreement. Are you sure you talked to Dan Harris?"

"Sounds like Gentle Ben with an attitude?"

Mercy chuckled. "That's the one."

"In that case, I have had the pleasure of speaking with Mr. Harris. His response was—*Grrrr.*" Nick's growl was low and menacing. "I took that as a no."

Laughing out loud, Mercy acknowledged the similarities between her station manager's rough, gravelly voice and Nick's growl. "I'd like to say he isn't usually like that, but lately I'm afraid he is."

"So, what do you say? You gonna help me, Mercy?"

"Sure," Mercy agreed without hesitation. "As long as you tell me why."

"Because you're a sucker for a good cause?" Nick tried hopefully, parroting what he'd heard her say on the phone.

"Wrong. Well, I am a sucker for a good cause. You got that right, but you answered the wrong question. What I want to know is why this is so important to Dr. Nick Devereaux."

"You mean besides giving me an excuse to meet *the* Mercy Malone?" he asked as if that privilege alone would be reason enough for a man to face any number of hardships.

"Stop fooling around, Nick," Mercy warned, raising her brow. "You're asking for a big commitment, and all I want to know is why you're doing this."

He rested his eyes for a moment and then dragged them open again, answering her as honestly as he could. "The unit functions, but I feel like I'm spinning my wheels sometimes. Before we even talk about additional medical equipment, you gotta know the physical layout's all wrong. The medprep is a small—I emphasize small—converted janitors' supply room. The waiting room's depressing as hell, and the nurses would give their eyeteeth not to have to tear the place apart to find a blood-pressure cuff small enough to give them an accurate pressure on a six-year-old."

Staggered by the very real frustration in his voice, Mercy asked, "Is it really that bad?"

"Worse. Oh, Mercy Hospital meets all the minimum standards, but there is a world of difference between minimum and adequate. A whole lot more between adequate and excellent."

Mercy worried her bottom lip with her teeth and readjusted the topaz ring she wore. Her conscience pinched her slightly because she hadn't visited the hospital or Sister Aggie in several years. "Will one hundred thousand dollars bring your emergency room up to excellent?"

"A lot closer," Nick allowed.

"What *will* it take?" Mercy pushed.

"More than we can raise with one fund-raiser."

"Fine. We'll do more."

"Hold on," Nick cautioned. "One step at a time. First, let's see if we can pull off this one. I don't want to turn Mercy Hospital into a trauma center. I just want to improve the emergency department that we've already got."

"What? No grand plan? No ambition?"

"Not anymore," Nick said bluntly, his reaction loaded with lessons learned from past mistakes.

"Sorry," Mercy said quietly. "I didn't mean to imply—"

"Yes, you did." His smile took the sting out of his words. "I've done my time in the big hospitals. It wasn't for me."

Mercy curled her legs beneath her. "Why?"

"Does it matter?"

"Only when I'm expecting a pop quiz from Sophie." Mercy grinned in an attempt to lighten his mood. "If you don't tell me, I'll have to make up something juicy."

"If I answer this, can we go back to fund-raising?"

"I suppose we can, but how am I going to be any help to you if I don't know anything about you or what you want? This is a perfectly reasonable line of questioning."

"Depends on your definition of reasonable."

Mercy heard the teasing note in Nick's complaint, but she also recognized a reluctance to talk about himself. While she idly traced the rolled seam of a couch cushion, Mercy said, "You hypocrite. You can dish it out, Dr. Devereaux, but you can't take it."

A cocky light in Nick's eyes disputed her statement very neatly and more strongly than words could have. Unswayed, Mercy refused to drop the subject. She'd managed to find a tiny hole in Nick's armor, and she intended to poke around a bit. "You love asking other people intensely personal questions, but you don't like coming under the microscope yourself. Now . . . why is that?"

"You really want to know why personal questions aren't my favorite questions to answer?" Nick asked, pinning her with a serious gaze, warning her that she might not like the answer.

"Yes. I do."

"Darlin', I'm out of practice at answering them, 'cause I don't have anyone who asks anymore."

Mercy immediately recalled the shadows in his eyes and the weariness she could feel beneath the surface in that brief moment at the kitchen table. She began to wonder why no one cared enough about Nick Devereaux to ask him personal questions. Lightly, she said, "I don't believe a word of that. I have eyes, Nick. I'll bet you have nurses swooning at your feet, asking *very* personal questions."

"If you believe that any of my nurses would swoon, you're sadly mistaken." He jerked forward as if shocked by an interesting thought and then settled into the nook formed by the chair back and wing. "*Bon Dieu*, you probably believe in love at first sight too."

"Hardly. I don't even believe in love at second sight!" Mercy scoffed, and realized her response was delivered much too sharply. *Damn!* How did a personal discussion about Nick end up being about her? Because he was better at this game than she was.

"Ah, no, *chère*, don't say that. Everyone believes in love."

"Not everyone. Not me. Now, lust I believe in, but love is—you'll excuse the expression—a pipe dream."

Nick templed his fingers over his abdomen and studied her solemnly, finally asking, "So which of the two scares you most? The consummation of lust or the possibility of love?"

Mercy sucked in a breath and wanted to throw something. Preferably at Nick. He lounged in that damn chair like a cat lazily watching a mouse that would soon be dinner. Surely he didn't expect an answer? An honest answer?

If he did, he'd have to wait until Miami averaged winter temperatures below freezing. She didn't answer, but she silently considered his question. Since she didn't believe in love, she obviously couldn't be scared of it, but she did tuck tail and run at the first sign of attraction. Lust scared the hell out of her, because lust invariably fooled people into believing in marriage and love.

She'd watched enough marriages wash up on the rocks to last a lifetime. Her own parents had significantly contributed to the wreckage piling up on the shore of divorce. Her father had been married three times, and her mother was just about to take the plunge for the fourth time. When this one sank like all the rest, Mercy would have to help her pick up the pieces one more time.

"You're stalling again," Nick told her.

"I'm thinking again!" she shot back. Sidestepping chemistry was the easiest way to avoid lust, and over the years she'd done a good job of picking and choosing whom she dated. If Mercy was more than mildly attracted to a man, she simply didn't go out with him. Unfortunately, Nick wasn't like the other men she'd politely sidestepped in the past.

He didn't appear to be satisfied with a pat on the head and being sent on his way. He liked to discuss things; he wanted answers and reasons. Nick obviously knew women, knew she ran from chemistry, and he seemed to think it was funny. Damn, that made her mad!

It wasn't as if she were a spinster who'd never had chances. She'd had chances! Lots of them. He had no right to waltz into her life and in a few short hours have her feeling as though she'd behaved like a coward—all because she hadn't been willing to take any of those chances.

"Come on, Mercy," he pressed gently. "You can tell me. What scares you? Lust . . . or love?"

"Doctors. Doctors scare me the most," she said, looking him straight in the eye. "Especially the ones who think they know absolutely everything about lust and love, which is impossible since they're generally too damn busy saving the world from disease and pestilence to notice much of anything beyond the hospital door!"

Unruffled, Nick said, "Don't you think that's a little harsh?"

"No." Mercy shook her head as she got up and tugged her white cotton shirt firmly over the waistband of her shorts. "My opinion is about on the money. You see, I'm an expert on doctors. My parents are doctors. All their friends are doctors. Every doctor I've ever met has one grand passion, and it's medicine. So don't sit there and shake your head, thinking I don't understand doctors. Or for that matter lust and love. Because neither do you, Dr. Devereaux. Your grand passion is medicine, not lust or love."

"You're wrong, Mercy."

"I don't think so. You want some coffee? I want some coffee. Don't get up."

"Black and strong enough to stand a spoon in,"

Nick instructed before she hightailed it out of the living room.

While he hated to see her go, he also knew he'd never make it back to Louisville unless he got some caffeine into his personal carburetor. When he closed his eyes to wait, he whispered softly, "Ah, Mercy, you may know everything there is to know about Louisville doctors, but what do you know about Cajun doctors?"

"Oh, for God's sake," murmured Mercy as she returned to the living room with two mugs of steaming French roast. She angled her wrist and checked the time. Nine-thirty.

Nick Devereaux slept peacefully in her favorite chair, arms dangling over the rests and legs supported by the cushioned footstool. Sleep softened the intensity of his expression, transforming him from gorgeously hard-edged to boyishly appealing. For once, Mercy found she could look her fill without having to face the amused glimmer in Nick's eyes.

When he'd put his shirt back on, he hadn't bothered to fasten the first couple of buttons. Tanned skin and the glitter of his gold chain contrasted sharply with the crisp white of his shirt, reminding Mercy of the thoughts that had run through her mind as he had stripped to the waist to fix her pipe. He might be irritating as hell, but he was one incredible piece of God's handiwork.

Mercy tiptoed around the sofa and set the cups down on the end table, using a news magazine as a coaster. Sighing didn't help much, but Mercy did it anyway. What was she supposed to do with the man?

Sending him out into the rainy, summer night with an hour's drive ahead of him seemed heartless and was probably dangerous as well. Nick hadn't complained of long shifts, but he was obviously bone-tired. Too tired to drive anywhere, her conscience added. Why else would he have collapsed so readily in the chair of a near stranger?

If she woke him, he'd be too stubborn to check into the local motel. No, Nick would drive back to Louisville, or die trying. However, the alternative was waking him up and suggesting that he spend the night with her. Ha! Mercy wouldn't willingly borrow that particular cup of trouble. It seemed her only choices were: Send him out into the rain, or let him sleep until morning.

He does look harmless enough now that he's asleep.

What a day, thought Mercy. First the flood. And then Nick Devereaux. Two disasters in one day. Resigned, she got up and pulled a light blanket from the downstairs closet and covered Nick. Even in sleep he took her breath away. His chiseled jaw showed the shadow of his beard, and his lashes were ridiculously thick and long. Without a doubt, Mercy knew, this man would make beautiful babies.

Too bad she wasn't in the market for a man to clutter up her life. Nick almost made her wish she were.

The first time she felt the featherlike touch, Mercy sleepily brushed at the sensation tickling her cheek without opening her eyes. She might even have recaptured sleep if her well-trained nose hadn't caught the scent of coffee, and when the touch turned into a gentle caress on her neck, realization ripped through her. Mercy's eyes snapped open just as she heard Nick Devereaux's smooth, creamy voice confirm her worst suspicions.

"Mornin', chère," he said as he rubbed his knuckles one last time down her neck and over the collarbone exposed by the loose T-shirt in which she slept.

He sat on the edge of the brass bed as though he brought her coffee every morning. Gone were the shadows beneath his eyes, and his shirt hung open all the way now. Now she could see that the small gold medallion on the diamond-cut chain was of St. Christopher, patron saint of children and travelers. Mesmerized by the need to find out if the medal was as warm as his body, Mercy reached up.

"Oh, for God's sake!" She snatched her hand back just in time.

Nick chuckled, but wisely said nothing.

Closing her eyes, Mercy counted calmly while dragging her hair away from her face. One . . . two . . . three . . . When she told Nick to get his butt out of her bedroom, she wanted to do it without anger. Four . . . five . . . six . . . She opened her eyes.

Struggling to maintain her composure, Mercy sat up, pulling the thin, satin-edged sheet with her. Although the old UCLA college T-shirt wasn't particularly revealing, she found herself wishing for a granny gown and a thick down comforter. Seven . . . eight . . . nine . . .

"You do take a while to focus on the world when

you wake up, don't ya, darlin'?" Nick asked with a sexy grin, and offered her the "dolphins are people too" mug.

. . . *ten*, she finished silently.

"Sometimes the world is pretty hard to take first thing in the morning," Mercy informed him as she plumped the feather pillows behind her. She took the coffee from his hand, but before she could coolly ask him to leave, Nick stood up and planted his hands on his hips.

"Pretty hard to take? Well, darlin', you'd better be ready to take whatever comes your way if you gonna let strange men sleep in your house and then leave your bedroom door unlocked!"

Frustrated because Nick had managed to make a good point, Mercy retaliated with, "I don't recall *asking* you to sleep over! You collapsed in my chair. What was I supposed to do with you? Put you in a car and let you kill someone when you fell asleep at the wheel? And I didn't lock my door because it doesn't lock!"

"Well, it should!"

"Well, it doesn't." Mercy sipped her coffee and glared at him. "I'm not stupid. I called the hospital and verified that you really do work there. The girl in Emergency was happy to talk about the charming Dr. Devereaux. But despite her assurances, if I'd known you weren't housebroken, I'd have barricaded the door! Where were you raised anyway? In a barn?"

"Close, darlin', real close. On the Bayou Teche in a little shack with a *galérie* across the front and rain on the tin patched roof."

The air Mercy had been storing up for her next

blistering retort sort of whooshed out. Quietly, she said, "That's no excuse for barging into my bedroom uninvited."

"I guess not, but you asked."

Silently, Nick admitted that invading her bedroom had been overstepping his welcome a bit, but truth be told, Mercy Malone was a magnet that drew him. The moment he entered her room and saw her sleeping, he'd felt his gut stirring with protective instincts as old as time. *Dieu!* This woman felt right. This house, this room felt right.

Like every other room in her house, her bedroom was filled with an odd collection of furniture, and each probably had a story. There was an old wood-and-leather domed steamer trunk, a small sheepskin rug at the foot of the bed, which he assumed was for the dog, a bentwood rocker, a skirted vanity table in front of a round gilt-framed mirror, and a full-length cheval mirror. A fancy interior decorator hadn't been anywhere close to this house, and all of it reminded him of home.

Mercy drank her coffee and stared at him, waiting for some act of contrition.

"I can see that I owe you an apology of sorts." Nick rubbed his neck again, pacing toward the door.

"Of sorts?" Mercy snorted and shifted her legs under the sheet. "How charming of you. I let you get some sleep—which you desperately needed, by the way—and the thanks I get is a lecture on safety tips for the single woman."

"The thanks you got was hot coffee in bed," Nick pointed out. "Although I don't know why you bother to drink such a weak excuse for coffee. It has no bite, no soul." He shook his head in disappointment. "That coffee can't warm a man that's been all day on the bayou, wet and chilled from a drizzle of rain. Next time I'll bring my own chicory blend and show you what a real cup of coffee tastes like."

"Next time?" As usual with Nick, Mercy found herself forgetting what she wanted to say and focusing on the time bombs he dropped into the conversation. *Next time he spent the night?*

That set off warning bells in Mercy's head. The only foolproof way to ensure that a relationship didn't turn nasty and bitter was never to start it in the first place. "Next time" wasn't a good sign. Phrases like "next time" were how relationships got started. Situations like this had to be dealt with ruthlessly. Mercy made what she thought was a valiant attempt to pretend nothing was happening between them.

She took a casual swallow from the mug and suggested, "Next time let's meet at the hospital. I really should see Sister Aggie anyway."

"Don't you worry. We're gonna meet in lots of places, *chère*," Nick assured her as he turned the crystal doorknob and pulled. "Places where you've never been. I promise you that."

"Where are you going? Wait—" Mercy ordered, but the master of innuendo was already out of her bedroom, and her gut told her he'd keep right on going out the front door. "Dammit!"

Quickly, she shoved the coffee onto her nightstand and flung off the covers. Racing to her closet, she grabbed a pair of black jeans and dragged them on while listening for the piercing screech of the screendoor hinge. She had to catch Nick before he left and make sure he understood that she only promised to help with the fund-raiser. Nothing else.

Mercy zipped on the run, and the screen door slammed closed behind Nick as she flew down the staircase. "Nick, wait! I cannot believe this. You can't just turn your back and walk away. I'm not through with you!" she called as she burst through the door.

Stopping on the bottom porch step, shirt still open, Nick turned. "Then that makes us even, *chère*. 'Cause I'm not through with you either. Not near through."

Nick swept back up the steps and pulled her against his bare chest in one motion. Shamelessly, he snuggled her body next to his, slowly making sure every possible inch of contact was made. The rush of sensation was incredible and Mercy didn't fight it. She leaned into the embrace, admitting to herself that she'd wanted this kiss since yesterday, since the first moment she'd gotten a look at his sensual mouth. For a heart-stopping moment she thought he was finally going to kiss her, but then he smiled and released her.

"Wave to Sophie," he advised as he descended the steps again.

He waved once at the older woman who was crossing the quiet tree-lined street and then walked calmly across Mercy's small yard to his glossy black Chevelle and got in. The engine kicked over instantly, sounding as rough and dangerous as Nick Devereaux. When the car pulled away from the curb, Mercy closed her mouth.

"Hello, dear!" Sophie shouted. "How's the plumbing?"

Mercy marveled at her neighbor's ability to completely ignore the fact that Nick's car hadn't moved a millimeter since last night, that he'd wandered out of her house at seven-thirty on a Sunday morning looking considerably worse for wear, and that he'd all but kissed her on the porch. "My plumbing's fine, but my nerves are completely shot."

"Oh, dear." The exclamation sounded more delighted than concerned, but Sophie climbed the steps and linked arms. "Then you've got to tell me everything. Is that coffee I smell?"

"Not according to Nick."

"Let's have some anyway, shall we?"

As she sat at the kitchen table, stirring her second cup of coffee, Mercy wished she could turn down the wattage on Sophie's bright yellow Mexican dress. The hem of this one was decorated with entwined blossoms in purple, turquoise, and pink. Sophie resembled nothing so much as a cheerful canary, and Mercy found the image distracting when she was trying to carry on a serious conversation.

Sophie—her sweet, gentle, grandmotherly neighbor—never directed a question at her that wasn't fully loaded. "So tell me, dear, is he good with his hands?"

A large gulp of coffee went down the wrong way, and Mercy grabbed for her napkin.

FOUR

When the coughing fit subsided, Mercy looked at Sophie through watery eyes and croaked, "Excuse me?"

"Is he good with his hands? On the phone you told me he was a doctor." Sophie rolled her eyes. "Some doctors just can't cope with the real world, you know. Did he take care of your plumbing problem with a minimum of fuss?"

Mercy breathed a sigh of relief, sniffed, and dabbed at her eyes. "Oh, that. He was very capable."

"Yes," agreed the older woman sagely. "He did strike me as the sort of fellow one could count on."

"I said he was capable. Not reliable."

"Isn't that the same thing?"

"Not even close."

Sophie set her cup carefully on the saucer, worry creasing her brow. "You don't sound as though you like the boy very much."

"Boy? Nick Devereaux can hardly be called a boy!

The word implies youth and uncertainty." Mercy tapped her fingernail against the cup edge. "I don't know how old Nick is, but he's years past being young and uncertain."

"Good. Then it's not totally hopeless." Sophie beamed and clasped her hands. "Joan and I were beginning to worry."

"Excuse me?" Mercy asked again, unable to keep the stunned expression off her face.

"Well, dear, we've tried to fix you up with every eligible male in these parts without much luck."

Mercy's mouth fell open. Finally, she sputtered, "You haven't! Tell me you haven't."

"Of course we have, dear. What are friends for?" Sophie patted her knee in an attempt to alleviate her distress. "We tried everyone—handsome, passable, widowers, even a few unemployed men. Only, you see, this is a small town. None of the men wanted to fail in front of his friends. You intimidated them."

"How could I intimidate them? I haven't even spoken to most of them!"

"That racy young woman you play on television intimidated them, dear. We tried to tell them that the woman on television isn't the real you, but men's egos are so fragile. All of them were positive you wouldn't give them the time of day, at least not after the first date. Especially the unemployed ones. Well, their loss is your doctor's gain," she finished encouragingly.

"He's not *my* doctor," Mercy argued lamely.

"Well, not yet, but I have hopes."

"No, you don't." Knowing she had to take control before Sophie began planning a fall wedding, Mercy told her the facts. "Nick slept in a chair last night.

He fell asleep, and I didn't have the heart to send him out in the rain. That's all there is to it. I'm sorry, but we didn't spend the night in wild passionate abandon. Nick Devereaux and I are not—I repeat not—romantically inclined. And even if he were, I wouldn't be."

"Oh, dear. This is going to be more difficult than I thought. Are you *sure* Nick isn't interested? He seemed awfully interested to me."

Mercy groaned and cradled her head in her hands for a moment. Snapping her head up and flipping long hair out of her face, she said, "Sophie, you're like family to me, and I appreciate your concern. But I am not looking for a man. I like my life. I like my job. Believe me. I meet men. If I wanted to date, I could."

"That's all very nice, dear. But is Nick interested or not?" Sophie persisted. "He seemed interested to me. The man drove all the way down here from Louisville, and he kissed you."

"He didn't come to see me, and he didn't kiss me! Actually he did, but he didn't."

"Well, which is it? Did he or didn't he kiss you?"

"He didn't kiss me, and he didn't come to see me. Not the way you mean." Drumming her fingers in an irritated rhythm, Mercy explained, "He works in Emergency at Mercy Hospital. He needs some help with a benefit for the hospital."

"Then he'll be back?" Sophie was obviously relieved.

"No, he won't."

Horrified, Sophie drew herself up. "You don't mean to tell me that you refused to help that gorgeous man after he fixed your plumbing?"

"I didn't turn him down!" Consciously, Mercy relaxed her jaw. "Even if he hadn't fixed my pipe, I would have said yes."

"Then why won't he be back?" Sophie demanded. "This whole thing doesn't make a bit of sense."

"He won't be back here because I'm going to make sure that all the details are taken care of in Louisville. I have no intention of encouraging a relationship with a doctor. I won't spend my days and nights waiting for a beeper to go off or the answering service to call. I moved to Haunt to get a little old-fashioned peace and quiet." Mercy gave Sophie a meaningful look. "I won't have any peace and quiet with Nick camping out on my doorstep."

"Trying to keep that Dr. Devereaux away from here is a bit like closing the barn door once all your horses have bolted, if you ask me."

Most of the time, Mercy adored Sophie. Now was not one of those times. "What's that supposed to mean?"

"It means that I don't think your Dr. Devereaux is going to play by your rules."

"He's not *my* doctor," Mercy corrected again.

"Well, he could be with just a little effort on your part," Sophie said firmly.

"This is too absurd," Mercy muttered.

She picked up her empty coffee cup and carried it to the sink with her. The view out the window was one of the reasons Mercy bought the house. An enormous crab-apple tree stood watch over her back fence. Now its branches were weighed down by thousands of rain droplets from last night's storm.

Finally and without looking around, Mercy said,

"One minute you're telling me that Nick's already interested—not that I care—and the next you're telling me that I need to make an effort if I want him! Sophie, if I was going to make an effort, it would be to scare Nick Devereaux off."

"Oh, dear! He doesn't look like the type who scares easily"—Sophie paused dramatically—"unless he's one of those men who only likes the chase and then doesn't know what to do once he's caught a woman. Do you think he's one of those?"

The quick denial died on Mercy's lips as she remembered that despite two golden opportunities, Nick hadn't kissed her. She'd been willing, and he hadn't kissed her. He sat on the edge of her bed this morning and didn't try anything. What made him hold back unless he was all bark and no bite?

On the porch this morning, he might have backed off because of Sophie, but what about last night in the kitchen? It was just the two of them, no witnesses. He'd made a flip excuse about fixing the pipe and turned away at the last second. Mercy stared out the window, wondering if Sophie was right. Wondering if her own initial impression of Nick had been wrong.

"It's so hard to tell about men," Sophie lamented from behind her. "Just to be on the safe side, don't wear your television outfits around him until he's more comfortable with you. I'm not criticizing, you understand, but some of those outfits could give a man performance anxiety. And there's always the fear that he may think you're too racy for a doctor to date. I'm sure he has his reputation at the hospital to consider."

Mercy smiled as she put her coffee cup in the sink.

Performance anxiety. If Sophie was right, wouldn't that wipe the smile off the doctor's face? Wouldn't it be nice to have the upper hand for once? She wondered which outfit would do the trick. "He did say something about a reputation," she said.

If Mercy had turned away from the window a moment sooner, she might have seen Sophie's satisfied expression, but by the time she looked at Sophie, her friend's brow was creased with concern. Sophie got up to leave. "You remember what I said now. None of those sexy outfits that are liable to give a man nightmares. Especially don't wear that practically indecent black shirt of yours."

Mercy Hospital looked like a huge, ugly, brick paperweight designed to keep the deteriorating neighborhood from blowing away in a breeze. A metal overhang covered the wide concrete stoop that fanned out from the front of the building. As Mercy walked through the glass doors she readjusted the thin shoulder strap of her black purse and smiled. She was actually looking forward to seeing Nick's face when he saw Midnight Mercy in person in all her glory.

Once she was inside the large foyer, memories assailed her. The hushed quiet of the common area was as familiar as the dying ficus tree beside the information center. Of course, the small tree couldn't possibly be the one she remembered, but the resemblance was uncanny. As she quickstepped past the information desk Mercy shot a question toward the woman's back. "Is the cafeteria still downstairs?"

Without looking up from her computer screen,

the woman pointed and said, "Unless they moved since this morning. Take the elevator down one floor and follow the main corridor. I wouldn't order the meat loaf."

Stifling a grin, Mercy said, "Thanks for the tip."

"You're welcome." The woman shoved a pencil behind her ear and grabbed the phone as it rang.

"Some things never change," Mercy murmured as she maneuvered around a yellow triangle inscribed with bright red words: CAUTION—WET FLOOR. Not trusting the traction of the soles of her high heels, she shifted her weight to the balls of her feet and hurried toward the bank of elevators.

She punched the arrow with the knuckle of her index finger as an elevator going down slid open. As the people emptied the elevator several of them did a double take with varying degrees of recognition in their faces. Mercy felt a moment's guilt over slipping quickly into the elevator without giving them a chance to pull out pens and ask the inevitable, "Say—aren't you . . . ?" But she rationalized her behavior with the excuse that she was late already. Twenty minutes late. The door finally whisked closed, and Mercy relaxed, blowing out a puff of breath.

"If you're gonna dress like that, *chère*, you gotta expect to sign a few autographs."

Mercy jumped and whirled away from the button panel to find Nick leaning nonchalantly in the corner of the wide elevator. Her first thought was that he looked tired and rumpled in his hospital scrubs, but her second thought was that he also looked dangerously sexy and could use a little tender loving care. When she caught her breath, she said, "Good God!

I thought this elevator was empty. Stop sneaking up on me!"

"I do not sneak," he answered as the elevator came to a stop and the doors opened.

"Oh, and what do you call that little scene in my bedroom?"

"Charming?" Nick asked much too innocently, and walked past her into the hallway.

As she turned to follow, Mercy choked back her response and replaced it with, "Why, Sister Agatha! How . . . how nice to see you again."

"It has been a while, hasn't it? You're looking . . . well." The tall silver-haired woman held out her hand to keep the elevator door from closing. In her pale blue linen suit, the nun appeared cool, well pressed, and completely in control. She looked every inch the authority figure Mercy remembered as she instructed, "But don't waste time greeting me, Mercy. Please continue your discussion. The five other people waiting for the elevator and myself are vastly curious about the little scene in your bedroom. If it wasn't charming, then what was it?"

"Nothing. It was nothing," Mercy assured her as she gingerly stepped out of the elevator. Suddenly the three-inch spike heels, her indecent blouse, and the Ultrasuede miniskirt no longer seemed like such a good idea. "Nick was inspecting my house for . . . for . . ."

"For trouble. I agreed to help with the remodeling of that old dinosaur she lives in," Nick supplied smoothly. "And we got into a heated discussion about old doorknobs and locks after I said I'd help."

"Really," the sister commented as she ushered the

group of hospital workers into the elevator with nothing more than a nod of her head. Sister calmly followed them in, but before she let the door slide shut, she said, "Mercy, I guess you're lucky to have Nick's help since he seems to know so much about bedroom doors and locks."

"Lucky, that's me," Mercy echoed with a wan smile, waiting for the door to close. When it finally did, she shook her head in disbelief. Rather than lucky, stupid seemed like a more appropriate description. She'd been so focused on scaring off the good doctor that she'd totally forgotten she'd probably have to face Sister Agatha in these clothes.

Knowing better than to laugh, Nick enjoyed the view while Mercy collected herself. He took his time, starting from the floor up. Heels did wonderful things for her legs. As a doctor, his opinion of high heels was pretty low. They were terrible for a woman's feet and back, but as a man, he appreciated the magic of flexed muscles and feminine curves. The soft fabric of her straight, rump-hugging skirt had one of those little open pleats in the back, and the see-through black blouse bared everything not covered by the skimpy black chemise she wore beneath it. He had no idea why she was barely dressed, but he liked her style.

Mercy caught him staring as she turned around. Fortunately, she remembered her game plan before she uttered one word about rudeness. That would have blown everything. If she wanted to convince Nick that pursuing her was a bad idea, first she had to convince him that she'd been ogled by better men than he and enjoyed it! She had to persuade him he'd bitten off more than he could chew. Midnight Mercy had to give Dr. Devereaux a case of performance anxiety so severe that he'd settle down and behave himself for the duration of their work on fund-raising.

Squaring her shoulders and trusting Sophie's instincts, she let a smile turn up the corners of her mouth. When she took a deep, slow breath and released it, Nick's eyes fell right where they were supposed to fall. They widened the tiniest fraction of an inch, and Mercy began to enjoy herself.

"I hope I didn't keep you waiting?" she asked, warming to her role and entwining her arm with his as they walked toward the cafeteria. Nick gave her a wary look, but said nothing as she continued, "I had an appointment at the station that ran late."

"I wasn't waiting," Nick confessed. He felt the firm round swell of her breast press into his arm as she swayed against him while they walked. Her blouse and chemise were so thin that the contact felt like flesh on flesh. "I got tied up with a patient."

"Ooh, tied up! That sounds like my kind of fun," Mercy purred, elated when she felt the muscles beneath her fingers tense. Encouraged by his instant reaction, she pressed on, "Whom do I call to get an appointment?"

Nick restrained the impulse to pull out his penlight and check her eyes for signs of substance abuse. Nothing else explained the transformation from reluctant girl-next-door to blatant seductress. The Mercy he'd met last weekend might not sweet-talk, but *this* one had just handed him an erotic image on a silver platter. If this woman had answered Mercy's door, Nick knew he'd have kissed her without hesitation. Kissed her and probably more.

"Midnight Mercy doesn't need an appointment," he assured her, wondering how far she intended to push this conversation. "All you have to do is say the word. I've memorized the Boy Scout book of knots, but I should warn you, Mercy. All my affairs are strictly BYOSS."

"Hmm. Affair. I like the sound of that." Disengaging her arm, Mercy entered the cafeteria and reached for a green plastic food tray. "Now what is BYOSS?"

"Bring your own silk stockings."

The tray almost slipped out of Mercy's fingers, but she managed to slide it onto the metal support. And Sophie was worried about shocking Nick? Worried about shocking a man who seemed perfectly comfortable standing in the middle of the hospital cafeteria, having a conversation about tying up his lovers with silk stockings? Although she was beginning to doubt her game plan, Mercy let her voice drop a bit and gave him her best provocative look. "Got a favorite color?"

"Darlin', if I have a choice, I prefer black, but I've got no objections to any color stockings you put on . . . as long as I get to peel 'em off. Real slow."

Mercy couldn't shake the picture forming in her mind. As clearly as if she were recalling an actual event, Mercy could feel his hands as they slipped beneath her skirt to toy with the edge of her stocking. She could feel his fingers as they grasped the garter and he released the clasp with one flip of his thumb.

The thought made her weak in the knees and heated her cheeks. This brilliant idea of hers was backfiring. Forcing herself to keep moving, she tossed her hair over her shoulder and stretched to reach the buckets of silverware behind the trays.

Nick knew he'd won their little sexual skirmish by the way she flushed and got busy. The idea of stripping Mercy had his own blood rushing around, too, but while Mercy's blood had gone to her cheeks, his had traveled south. Watching her skirt rise several inches as she reached for utensils didn't help Nick's state of arousal. He couldn't remember being this hard for a woman he'd never kissed.

Every moment in her company added to his conviction that Mercy kept an incredibly sensual nature under lock and key. He began to wonder if she was afraid to give in to lust unless she was acting a part, a part like Midnight Mercy. She could vamp to her heart's content and never have to deliver, since most men would be shaking in their boots at the thought of making love to an experienced woman who might expect them to tie her up.

Stunned, Nick slid his own tray onto the cafeteria counter and realized why Mercy had called and asked for a lunch date. She actually thought she could scare him off with this sex-hungry act of hers! As far as he was concerned, she could try all she wanted. It wasn't gonna happen. "So, *chère*, are we on for Saturday night?"

To give her hands something to do besides shake, Mercy reached for a bowl of strawberries and peaches in a rich red sauce. "Why don't I check my schedule and get back to you?"

The late-lunch crowd began to line up behind them, so Nick simply said, "Why don't you check your supply of stockings, and I'll get back to you?"

"Whatever." Mercy shrugged as though she didn't care, although she was edgy as hell on the inside. *Damnation!* Sophie had made intimidating men sound so easy. Nick didn't look the least bit scared. In fact, the plan was backfiring so badly that she was the one with performance anxiety. Trying to shake the feeling that she was in over her head, Mercy concentrated on filling her tray.

Nick followed Mercy to a corner booth. "Good choice. A quiet spot for a cozy chat is just what I had in mind."

Before Mercy could reply, a mountainous orderly approached her, shyly asking her to sign a crumpled Dodgers baseball hat that he pulled out of his back pocket. Mercy smiled to put the big man at ease and chatted briefly about the team's pennant chances before she signed the autograph. When the orderly had gone, she echoed Nick's comment from the elevator. "I think you can forget your cozy chat. When I'm dressed like this, you gotta expect me to sign a few autographs."

"I don't mind. I like watching you smile at people. But it also makes me wonder if you like being a celebrity."

"Who wouldn't?" she asked, implying his ridiculous question didn't deserve an answer. "So many men. So little time."

"Oh, I don't know who wouldn't like being a celebrity." Nick flipped a napkin across his lap and added, "Unless it was maybe someone who lives in a small sleepy town an hour's drive from Louisville?"

"Don't tell me you haven't already figured out why I bought a hundred-year-old house in Haunt,

Kentucky?" Mercy's blue eyes twinkled at him, reminding him that beneath the sexy-bombshell routine, she was still a very real woman who didn't take herself too seriously. Even when she was trying to scare a man off.

"I'm sure you want everyone to think it's for publicity."

"Of course it's a colossal public-relations ploy! One of the people at the station suggested it a couple of years ago when I said I was ready to take the plunge and become a home owner. I'm only at the station a couple of days a week, so what could be more perfect for a horror-show queen than a spooky house in Haunt, Kentucky?"

"Then how come nobody knows that's where you live?"

"I like it that way," Mercy answered honestly, and poked a piece of fried okra with her fork. "When I got to know the people, I decided I didn't want the place turned into a zoo every Halloween by the publicity people."

With sudden certainty, Nick knew that the little town with the catchy name had become Mercy's haven. The need for privacy was a concept that he understood all too well. He also knew the trap privacy could become. Little by little he had forgotten how much he needed people until the silence in his life began keeping him up at night, forcing him to get away from Louisiana and away from the memories of the family he'd lost.

As they ate he thought about Mercy's privacy and wondered who she was trying to keep away. Couldn't be the fans. She wasn't the least upset with the orderly

for interrupting their lunch. And it couldn't be her
neighbors. Sophie and Joan obviously didn't feel any
need to keep their distance. That left family and men.
Neither was a subject on which Mercy had volunteered any details.

"I believe you like your privacy so much you're
hidin' out in Haunt," he said finally. "Can't be that
many eligible men living there, and my guess is that
your parents don't get down too often. I didn't realize
you were a coward, *chère*."

Mercy's mouth fell open. "I am not hiding out!
And why are we dissecting my life again? I thought
we'd already done that once."

"And it was such fun, I thought I'd do it again."

"Let's not."

"Coward," Nick accused as he speared a piece of
roast beef.

Sitting back, Mercy realized that she'd totally
abandoned the sexy I-can-handle-anything posture.
Nick did that to her. He made her forget to "act"
and made her react to him instead. Being called a
coward stung her more than she wanted to admit.
Maybe because in the past she had accused herself
of being an emotional coward whenever she stepped
away from relationships that showed promise. After
growing up in the war zone of her parents' lives, she
just couldn't bring herself to believe in forever.

They ate in silence for a few minutes until Mercy finally asked, "Do you dissect all the women you
meet? I mean, does this charming routine of yours
actually work on women?"

"It's worked on you. You called me for lunch."

"I called about the fund-raiser," she snapped. "Not

just to see you. I wanted to tour the emergency room and get a feel for what you need to do here!"

"You got my permission to feel anything you want," he offered as he pushed his plate away and hooked an arm over the top of the booth. His eyes dropped to the shadow of cleavage exposed by the sheer material and the low-cut piece of lingerie beneath it. "You always dress this way for charity work?"

"I thought this was why you wanted me!"

"That's exactly why I want you."

"I meant for the fund-raiser!"

"I did too."

"You did not!" Mercy's frustration showed in her voice and the way she wadded up her napkin.

"There you go again, darlin'. Mistaking everything I say."

"The only mistake I made was in thinking you had enough sense to back off like all the other insecure men Sophie's tried to fix me up with!"

"Mercy, I don't back down from a challenge, especially when it's obvious my opponent is running a bluff." He reached across the table and dragged his thumb across her bottom lip, rubbing away the red stain of strawberry sauce. Deliberately, Nick paused to suck the pad of his thumb and then said, "I was born with a deck of cards in one hand and a pair of dice in the other. I'm a Cajun, *chère*. Gamblin' is a way of life. I could shuffle a deck and play cutthroat bourré before I could read and write."

Mercy barely heard a word he said after he stroked her lip. With an effort, she resisted the temptation to run her tongue along the path his thumb had taken. She knew she should be angry, but she wasn't sure at whom: Herself for misjudging her ability to intimidate the man, or Nick for allowing her to make a fool of herself with this charade. Letting go of her anger, she asked, "When did you figure it out?"

Before he answered, he leaned back, a section of his black hair falling against his forehead. "Right about the time I realized the idea of my peeling stockings off your incredible legs was as exciting to you as it was to me."

"I wasn't excited. I was . . ." Mercy didn't bother to finish the sentence. Telling Nick that her face flushed because she was "hot" was not going to help her case.

"Oh, you were excited all right. I don't think a bad girl on the prowl would go up in flames at the thought of being stripped. And you went up in flames, *ma jolie fille*."

"Don't call me that."

"My pretty girl?"

"Whatever it means, don't call me that. Or *chère*. Or darlin'. I'm not interested, Nick. All I want to do is get this fund-raiser planned and get back to fixing up my house."

"Before it falls down around your ears?"

She ignored him. "Before I make a really big mistake and listen to my hormones."

As he scooped up their tickets Nick asked, "And what's wrong with listening to your hormones?"

"Because it would be asking for trouble." Mercy slid out of the booth, brushing aside Nick's offer of help.

Nick let her go, stopping long enough to pay the check, and then joined her at the elevator. "I've been called a lot of things, *chère*, but never trouble."

"Can we drop this?" Mercy asked. "Just give me the tour and then let's go see Sister Agatha about this damn party so I can clear the details with the station."

"Is that going to be a problem?"

A secret smile hovered on Mercy's lips. "Not if Dan wants me to consider staying in Louisville instead of taking Pittsburgh's offer when my contract comes up this fall."

Nick frowned and let her precede him into the elevator. No wonder she was in such a hurry to get her house in shape. She wanted to be able to sell it quickly if necessary. "You're thinking about leaving Louisville?"

"Maybe," was all she'd say. "Pittsburgh is a much bigger television market. Means more exposure."

Eyeing her outfit with speculation in his gaze, Nick said, "I don't think you have that much left to expose."

After Mercy signed autographs for the staff on duty, the tour went quickly. The department was quiet, and the physical layout was limited. As they walked through the unit together she realized that, in his element, Nick was different, all business.

No, she decided, detached was the word she was looking for, as though he disconnected his emotions when he stepped into the ER. She had trouble reconciling the man at her side with the charmer who'd fixed her sink and slept in her chair. Believe it and get over it, she warned herself. He was a doctor just like her parents, and she should be thankful for the wake-up call.

No matter how much she'd like to believe he was different, he wasn't. If a patient died, he would wash his hands and go on to the next one. He could probably cut off his feelings as easily as he could take off a coat.

"Everything looks so old," Mercy commented, getting her thoughts off Nick and back on the hospital.

"With good reason. Most of it is. Take a good look at the ceramic tile on the walls. You can always tell how old a hospital is by the number of broken ceramic tiles on the emergency-room walls."

"I don't think you have a tile without a crack in it!"

"Proof positive that the ER could use a little good-will in the form of cold hard cash," he said. "God knows the waiting room needs an overhaul."

Mercy immediately agreed. The dreary waiting room did nothing to calm the shredded nerves of family members anticipating the worst. Several of the nurses joined them, and after they added their perspective, Mercy's head was spinning with a hundred ideas for how a well-spent chunk of money could improve Mercy Hospital. Nick unbent long enough to contribute a couple of dozen ideas of his own and even some jokes.

After he paged and spoke to Sister Agatha, Nick led the way out of Emergency. "She'll meet us at her office."

"Who gets to decide how the money will be spent?"

Mercy asked. "You said something about a bigger medprep room, and the nurses are all for converting to the more modern drug carts."

Nick rubbed the faint stubble of beard that shadowed his jawline. "If I have my way, it'll be a joint effort between the community, administration, and the medical personnel. Sister said something about getting a community users' group to help. The only thing I'm dead set against is hiring a fancy consulting firm to give an opinion that'll cost several thousand dollars."

"Good Lord, the last thing you need is to pay for opinions you can get for free around here. Everyone on staff seems to know exactly what would improve the situation!"

"That's putting it mildly," Nick said with a shake of his head. "When you feel like a little hamster in a squeaky wheel, going round and getting nowhere, you know exactly where to put the oil. The nurses have been spinning in that squeaky wheel a lot longer than I have. I appreciate your letting them blow off a little steam."

Grinning, Mercy said, "No problem. If I was trying to save lives in an environment designed forty years ago, I'd be doing something a little more obnoxious than blowing off steam. It amazes me how you can function without enough space to do the job right."

Nick rapped on Sister Agatha's office door and then shot her a knowing look. "Personally, tight spaces have never bothered me."

A half sigh, half groan escaped Mercy. This was the Nick she was used to, and she bit her tongue rather than say anything he could twist into another subtle reminder of the sensual undercurrents flowing around them. Of all the men who could have arrived on her doorstep and set off a hormonal chain reaction, why did it have to be a doctor?

At Mercy's warning look, he laughed and knocked again. "When I paged her, Sister said we should wait in her office if she wasn't back when we arrived. She's stuck talking to the honorable Mrs. Oliver Reed, the wife of Dr. Reed, whose degree is administrative, not medical. He's a member of the hospital board, and Mrs. Reed likes to use that fact to create trouble." Finally, he opened the door. "Looks like Sister could be a while. Can you wait?"

"Yeah." Mercy entered the semidark office. "You make talking to Mrs. Reed sound like a fate worse than death."

"No, a conversation with Dr. Reed is a fate worse than death. He's a sixty-five-year-old, narrow-minded prude who thinks the cure for sexually transmitted diseases is a nickel between the knees and a little willpower." He shut the door as Mercy deposited her purse in one of the brown upholstered chairs in front of Sister Agatha's desk. "By contrast, his wife is just a mildly unpleasant trip into an alternate universe."

Intrigued by Nick's characterization of the Reeds, Mercy turned and leaned against the top of the chair. "Is this idle gossip about the man or have you had the pleasure of speaking with Dr. Reed?"

Nick reached for the lights and flipped them on, revealing a neat, well-organized office. "I'm not sure I'd call it a pleasure, but I have actually talked to Dr.

Reed and his wife. I talked to all the board members before I approached the station about the fund-raiser." He leaned against the gray metal door, one hand on the knob and the other on his hip.

"Sounds like you did a little more than talk to Dr. Reed. Tell me the truth. What did he say that sounded your horn?"

"Nothing in particular."

"Yeah, right. Then tell me in generalities," Mercy pressed, and walked toward him. "This has got to be good. I want to know what makes you angry."

"You might not like it, *chère*."

"I'll risk it."

"Dr. Reed believes this little fund-raiser is in poor taste. He doesn't think we should be linking the hospital's good name with something as tawdry as a brainless television sexpot."

"Brainless!" Mercy exploded. Sexpot she could let pass, but to be called brainless burned her up. She spent a great deal of time and energy researching each of the movies on her show. While she had to live with whatever movie package the program exec negotiated each year, she did everything she could to lift her show above the average and give her viewers a little something extra. "I do not look or act brainless."

"Mercy, I believe Dr. Reed is more concerned with your bust measurement and how much cleavage shows than he is concerned with your IQ."

Indignant, she put her hands on her hips. "I hope you told him to take a long walk off a short pier."

"That came later."

"There's more?"

"Let's just say he discovered that I'm not interested in his views on celibacy, or where I should draw the line in my intimate relationships."

"Where do you draw the line?" asked Mercy, suddenly realizing that his answer was very important to her.

Nick took a step toward her, stopping a few inches away. Mercy looked like a woman waiting for bad news, standing very still, very quiet. Her sheer black shirt teased him with the soft curves that lay beneath the filmy veil. Dragging his gaze to her face, he knew better than to answer the wrong question. "Are you asking me how many women I've slept with, or are you asking me about the variety of my sexual experience?"

Appalled that she continued to fall into such intimate conversations, Mercy stammered an apology. "I'm sorry, Nick. It's none of my business."

Nick caught her elbow before she could back away. Without saying anything, he urged her closer, adjusting his legs to fit her snugly in the cradle of his thighs, even though her upper body leaned away from him. "But it is your business, *chère*. One of these days you and I are going to end up in bed together. You know it, and I know it. It's only a matter of time."

"I don't know that," Mercy argued, but the words were too shaky to be confident.

"I do, and I'm sure enough for both of us. Sure enough to wait until you know it too."

"You'll be waiting a long time."

"What are you afraid of, *chère*? Me? Or you?"

"I'm not afraid." But even as she said it her body called her a liar. Her stomach flipped the moment his palms rubbed along her arms, up to the shoulder and down to her elbows. Ever so slowly, he bent toward her, bringing his face closer as if to tell her a secret.

"Coward," Nick accused softly, his words ruffling the hair at her temple.

Mercy closed her eyes, trying to fight the impulse to lean into his broad chest. "Stop calling me that."

"Stop being one. All you have to do is kiss me."

A sensation of excitement shivered through her. Nick dropped feathery kisses on her forehead, cheeks, and nose, inching closer to her mouth with every brush of his lips. All of her senses were screaming for him just to kiss her and get it over with, to take the decision out of her hands. But Nick wouldn't do that. He continued to tease her with tiny nibbles designed to drive her crazy.

Every touch silently called her a coward. When his mouth began to slide down her neck, she sagged against him. She hadn't wanted the small sigh of satisfaction to escape, but it did. Nick worked his way back up the column of her throat, his hands never leaving her arms, never crushing her to him or exploring her body. All he took were small soft bites of tender flesh. Toying with her. Playing with her.

Finally, with his mouth hovering over hers, he asked, "What'sa matter, *chère*? Can't make up your mind?"

The tension inside Mercy coiled more tightly, demanding release. She surrendered and pressed her mouth to his.

FIVE

When she opened her mouth beneath his, Nick swept his tongue inside, sampling her sweetness, tasting the trace of peaches. The simple shift of her body as her arms crept around his neck forced a groan from him because her breasts replaced her hands on his chest. Her softness bore into him, a feminine counterpoint to the hardness in him.

The feel of her pressed against him produced an instinctive reaction, a need to feel her body beneath his fingers. Nick's hands slid down to her waist and over the curve of her rump. Knowing the edge of her skirt was only inches from his fingertips excited him. He cupped her derriere, letting his palms soak up the velvety texture of the material as he aligned his lower body more perfectly with hers.

Mercy couldn't remember a kiss like this one. A kiss that pulled at her soul and had heat pooling in her belly. When Nick pressed the ridge of his hardness against her, she felt the spark of a long-forgotten need. Raising on her toes, she rubbed against him, slowly lowering herself, deliberately teasing his erection. She'd forgotten the wonderful anticipation that could flow through her veins in a heated rush. She'd forgotten how easily lust could seduce her.

At the discreet cough from the doorway, Nick suddenly remembered that he was thoroughly kissing Mercy in the office of a nun. Although his closed eyes flew open, he broke the embrace as gently as possible. Nick could feel Sister Agatha's gaze boring into his back, but couldn't resist capturing Mercy's bottom lip with his mouth one last time before he set her away from him. He wanted to take some time to enjoy the satisfied and dazed look in her blue eyes when she finally opened them, but Sister Agatha was waiting and watching. Carefully, he moved his hands as the sister coughed again.

"Oh no," Mercy whispered as she landed back in reality.

"*Mais yeah, chère.*"

The nun shut the door behind her and crossed the room. As she dropped a couple of manila file folders onto the large calendar pad that protected most of her desktop, she said, "I hope I'm not interrupting anything important."

Totally unrepentant now that he'd regained his composure, Nick gave the older woman a grin he hoped was irresistible. "Depends on your point of view."

"Nick, please. You're not helping," Mercy said. She hadn't been in the same room with Sister Aggie in years, but she felt like it was yesterday. Without much luck, she tried to divorce herself from the memories of a nineteen-year-old girl facing an authority figure she respected. Years of conditioning prompted the racing of her heart and the need to apologize. "Sister, this is your office, and we shouldn't have . . . well, I'm sorry if we offended you."

"I'm not the least offended, Mercy. Or easily shocked, which you should remember. I simply wanted to know if this was an important kiss or just an indiscreet display of infatuation." Sister Agatha sat down behind her desk and motioned them to follow suit.

Mercy settled into a chair and braced herself, knowing that an old indiscretion was about to be dredged up.

"You always were an impetuous girl, but I would have thought you'd learned your lesson the first time you kissed a doctor in my office."

"The *first* time?" Nick asked as he sat down on Mercy's right. He shifted in his chair for a better view of both women, but he addressed his question to Mercy. "I thought you didn't like doctors."

"I'm older and wiser," Mercy said. She kept her tone casual, making a joke of the situation. "I had a crush on one of the residents. He was gorgeous, but I had to give up on him when I discovered he couldn't kiss worth a"—Mercy stumbled and finished—"darn."

"You gave up on him when you realized that he was just like your parents," the sister corrected. "All medical talk and no action. You've never had any patience with doctors. Not that you had any business playing doctor back then."

"It was one innocent kiss!" Mercy informed both of them, and curled her fingers around the chair arms. The urge to throttle Nick was almost unbearable.

Although he didn't actually call her a liar, he conveyed that impression by shrugging and leaning back with his legs stretched out in front of him. With an effort, Mercy regained her poise and asked, "Could we please drop the subject of my adolescent exploits and get back to the present?"

"The present? Let me see . . . that would be today's not-so-innocent kiss?" Sister clasped her hands together on top of the manila folders in the middle of her desk, appearing to possess all the patience in the world as she waited for an answer.

Caught between the nun's perceptive gaze and Nick's obvious amusement, Mercy decided she was outnumbered. Sometimes the best defense was a well-organized retreat. "Maybe we should discuss the fundraiser?"

To her surprise, Sister Agatha agreed. "Before we start, would either of you like some coffee? A soda?" She paused and glanced toward Mercy's chest before raising her eyes to Mercy's face. "Perhaps a coat for you? The air-conditioning has made this room a bit chilly."

Time stopped, and heat flooded her cheeks. She didn't need to look down to know that her nipples were alert and clearly outlined by the sheer fabrics she wore. Mercy truly understood the expression "I just wanted the earth to open up and swallow me." That's exactly how she felt. She wanted to crawl under a rock.

Nick, on the other hand, was enjoying himself tremendously. Well, she'd be damned if she'd make a fool of herself by gasping and covering up like a silly schoolgirl caught in her underwear. As casually as she could, she angled her foot and managed to give the snickering doctor a kick in the ankle. To the nun she said, "No, I'm fine. Really."

"All right." The nun watched with interest as Nick leaned down to rub his leg. "I assume that Nick has already shown you our emergency department?"

"She got the nickel tour," Nick confirmed, and straightened. "Right now that's about all it's worth."

"In my opinion, it's worth less than a nickel," Mercy told them bluntly. "Working in that ER has to be like working in a dungeon. There aren't any windows to the outside, and that old, stale smell is the medical equivalent to the smell in a mildewy, musty old house. No matter how much you clean it, you'll never be able to get the smell out."

The older woman pushed her chair back from the desk a little bit. "We haven't had the money to spend on the ER, but Nick tells me you're going to help us change that."

"Absolutely. I'll even admit to a soft spot for the hospital." Mercy began to relax now that the conversation was on safer ground. She'd given a lot of thought to Nick's request and to why her manager had turned down Mercy Hospital. "The only question left is are you willing to do what it's going to take to get the station's support?"

"What do you mean?" Nick asked. "I thought you said the television station's support wasn't going to be a problem."

"It won't be. If we're smart." Mercy looked first at the sister and then at Nick. "Are you open to suggestions?"

When they both nodded, she continued. "Let me

explain a few things. The only reason the FCC grants television licenses is for the public benefit. That means every station that wants to keep its license had better be doing its part for the community and the public good."

"Then why wouldn't your station manager meet with me about this project?" Nick asked.

Mercy motioned with her hand to indicate that she was getting there. "I've done a little checking and I've come up with a couple of reasons. One has to do with me, and the other has to do with the scope of this project."

"What have you got to do with this?" Sister interrupted. "There's no conflict of interest. Your parents aren't on staff anymore."

Mercy bent forward. "It's nothing like that. I'm in the last year of my three-year contract. Dan, the station manager, found out that a station in Pittsburgh has contacted my agent. Consequently, he'd rather not do anything that might increase my popularity. He's afraid it would encourage Pittsburgh to make me an offer I couldn't refuse."

"All he has to do is match the offer if he wants to keep you," Nick countered.

"He can't wave a magic wand and make Louisville a bigger television market. That's what the issue is. Not money, but the opportunities that come when a personality moves to a bigger market. A bigger market means getting noticed by syndicators, and that could mean feeding the show to several markets. Eventually maybe a cable deal."

"Right." Nick nodded and realized he understood Dan's dilemma. He didn't much like the idea of Mercy moving away for career advancement either. "You told me this part. Pittsburgh means more exposure."

"Exactly." Mercy pushed her hair away from her face and settled back in her chair.

"So where does that leave us," Sister asked.

"In the driver's seat." Mercy grinned. "Dan's plan was great as long as I didn't find out about it. But now I know, so it's going to be a little more difficult to ignore your request."

"Okay, so what do we do at this point?" Nick asked.

"The scope of the project is all wrong. We need to think bigger."

"Bigger isn't better." Nick shook his head forcefully. "It's just more trouble. I told you we didn't want to turn this place into a trauma center. We're a plain ordinary little hospital. All we want to do is some remodeling."

Sister Agatha added, "I agree. We don't want this getting out of hand."

"Don't get excited," Mercy advised calmly. "Let me give you a few facts before you shoot this benefit in the foot. You're planning an event for one thousand people, right?"

"At a hundred dollars a plate, that'll give us enough money to get started." Nick repeated what he'd outlined before.

"After expenses, all you'll have is maybe seventy-five thousand dollars," Mercy told him. "A thousand people is small potatoes to the station, not even one percent of the population in Louisville. To make matters worse, television stations think in terms of households. So take that thousand and divide it in two. That's five hundred couples."

She turned to Sister Aggie. "According to Nick's plan, he wants the television station to kick in valuable airtime to run the promo, to foot the bill for the production cost of the promo, *and* he wants the station to let someone host my show for an evening. Do you really think the station's going to go to all of this trouble to reach five hundred households?"

Sister argued, "But this will benefit the whole area around the hospital. The patients and their families will be more comfortable. The doctors and nurses will have an easier time doing their jobs."

"You can sell a thousand tickets with print ads and radio spots."

"But the television angle would bring in more donations," Nick contended.

"Sure. But the station's position is going to be that they could utilize that airtime more effectively and help more people by running PSAs—public-service announcements—on blood pressure, AIDS, fire-safety tips, and a million other topics. Ask yourself this question: How is the station going to do more good? By getting five hundred couples involved in your project, or by using that airtime to alert fifty thousand people to the danger of high blood pressure, the silent killer?"

When she finished, both Nick and Sister Agatha were frowning and silence hung heavy in the room.

"I see your point," the older woman acknowledged. She tilted her head and studied Mercy for a moment before she asked, "I know you, young lady. You've got a plan, or you wouldn't have come here today. Don't keep us in suspense any longer. What do you suggest?"

"First we have to bump the attendance."

"By how much?" Nick asked.

"Double it. Make it two thousand people at two hundred dollars a head." Mercy paused for a moment while she let that sink in. Then she added, "There are a couple of hotels in the city that can handle a function this big."

"Big is the key word," Sister Agatha repeated, and warned Nick, "This whole fund-raiser is your idea. If we go forward with this project, I'll expect you to handle the monster you've created."

"You can count on me, Sister. I don't start something unless I'm willing to go all the way. So you have my word. I am absolutely ready, completely willing, and more than able to do anything necessary." He sent Mercy a sinful glance as he said, "What I want to know is if I can count on Mercy to do the same?"

As usual, Nick's conversation sounded so innocent on the surface, but Mercy's pulse fluttered as his little speech sank in. Was there no shame in the man? They were sitting in a nun's office, for Pete's sake! And he was brazenly putting her on notice that he was going to finish what had been started with that kiss.

Carefully avoiding his dark eyes, Mercy said, "Sister, you know I'll do everything I can."

"That's good enough for me," Nick declared.

"Before we pat each other on the back, I should warn you that we have to agree on a couple more issues," Mercy interrupted.

"There's more bad news?" Nick asked with a sigh.

"This event has to be high profile. Fun with a kick.

Sedate won't get it. Not if you intend to appeal to the audience of *The Midnight Hour*."

A ghost of a smile hovered on Sister Agatha's lips. "I would have thought that an evening with Mercy Malone would be exciting enough for most people."

"Works for me," Nick volunteered in the earthy accent that sent chills up Mercy's spine.

She looked toward Nick and narrowed her eyes, daring him to say one more word. He got the message, and she turned back to the sister. "You'd be surprised how fickle the public is. You're going to have to wine 'em, dine 'em, and dance 'em. I'm not suggesting something . . . tawdry," she finished, choosing Dr. Reed's charming description of her television persona. "But we'll need a theme. Something that fits my image. Are you okay with that?"

"I don't disapprove of you or your show, if that's what you're asking," the nun assured her. "I seem to recall that most of your horror movies revolve around the theme of good versus evil with good always winning in the end. So I think I can safely leave that decision to you and Nick once the other details are worked out."

"Okay. That brings me to the last change we need to make. Nick said something about a community organization helping us out."

"Sister thought we could use all the help we could get," he explained.

"She's right," Mercy agreed. "I was going to suggest we find a group to support this project, but it seems that Sister Aggie is two steps ahead of me. As usual." She grinned at her, acknowledging the nun's sharp mind. "The station does more than enough public service work to satisfy the FCC. So we need that little something extra in our corner. Is this group you've scrounged up willing to be an active sponsor? Get in there and get their hands dirty? We could really use someone with benefit experience."

"I don't know about benefit experience. Kentucky Parents for Better Health Care is a relatively new organization, but they're committed to providing better care for low-income households," Sister Agatha informed her. "Since most of our client base falls in that group, I gave them a call as soon as Nick brought his idea to me. From what I gathered during the conversation, they'll be as active as you want."

"Great. Now what about the time line?" Mercy asked, turning to Nick. "When did you want to throw this party?"

"As soon as possible. How long does it take to put something like this together? Six months?"

"Usually, but that's too long for me. I'd like to get this over and done with before negotiations on my contract begin."

"When's that?"

"Probably September."

Nick whistled and shot an uncertain look at the nun.

To nudge them along, Mercy added, "If we can find the right hotel and press hard, could we pull that off?"

"Middle of August?" The nun and Nick voiced the question in unison. They continued to gaze silently at each other, obviously weighing the pros and cons of rushing the event.

"I know that's only about ten weeks, but I've got

favors with advertising people I can call in," Mercy promised them. "Once we decide on a theme, we can have the print ads worked up in just a few days. We wouldn't have to do anything fancy for the television promo. In fact, it would be better if we used my set."

Nick shrugged and admitted, "I've got the time to put into this project. Nothing else and nobody on my schedule. If Mercy says we can get it done, then I'm willing to try."

Smiling, Mercy said, "All right then. It looks like we have a fund-raiser to put together. I'll set up a meeting with Dan for next Monday afternoon."

Mercy heard the rumble of Nick's Chevelle through the open window of the office she'd converted from a spare bedroom. Although her heart was already skipping beats, it wasn't until the car door shut that the black Labrador picked up her head and paid attention.

The engine rumble had meant nothing to her dog, but Witch associated the slamming of car doors with the weekly delivery of videotape from the station. Since the young Zip Transit driver always had an extra minute to scratch her chin, Mercy wasn't surprised when Witch jumped off the roomy sofa. With a welcoming woof, the dog joyously dashed out of the room and down the stairs.

Briefly, Mercy considered ignoring the sharp buzz of the doorbell, only to discard the idea. Pulling off a pair of designer tortoiseshell and wire-rim glasses, Mercy sighed and slowly leaned over to place them on a shelving unit full of movie trivia books. Resigned, she reached for the remote control and switched off the VCR machine. Her home office served as more than a place to put a desk and a file cabinet.

Across from the comfortable sofa placed along one wall was the big-screen TV she used to preview each week's horror movie as she prepared her monologue and comments for the show. She'd been just about to watch next week's movie, but work would have to wait until after she'd dealt with Nick's invasion.

She hadn't been alone with Nick since the kiss. Lady Luck had delivered a small reprieve at the end of their meeting. Nick had been paged to Emergency. Before he left the room, his eyes let her know that the reprieve was only temporary and she could expect him to come calling. In fact, she had expected him long before Sunday afternoon.

The doorbell rang again, sounding more impatient this time, although she knew it was technically impossible for a doorbell to have feelings. As she left the room Mercy placed the remote on top of the television. Witch met her at the landing, thumping her tail against the stair rail and encouraging Mercy to hurry. As the dog raced back down the steps Mercy told her, "Settle down. It's not who you think it is."

Witch didn't seem to care. To a friendly dog, any visitor was cause for celebration. Uncharitably, Mercy hoped that Nick hated dogs—or at least that dogs hated him. As soon as she opened the door, her hopes were dashed. Nick stood on her porch bouncing a pink neon tennis ball obviously intended as a bribe for Witch. The doctor's grin advertised the fact that he was quite pleased with himself for remembering that her dog was probably home by now.

"I suppose you think that's going to be enough to get you in the door?" Mercy asked as she grabbed the Lab's collar to stop her bouncing in unison with the tennis ball.

"Of course not." Nick caught the ball as it sprang up off the wooden porch and held it, drawing her attention to the flex of his arm muscles as they strained against the sleeve of his black T-shirt. With his other hand, he grasped something draped over his shoulder. Slowly, he pulled a pair of black silk stockings free. "I brought a toy for you too."

Only a man as brazenly confident as Nick would arrive on a woman's doorstep, unannounced and bearing lingerie. Mercy's mouth dried out, and she had to lick her lips and swallow before she could say anything. When she finally found her voice, she confessed a secret, "Then you wasted your money, because neither Midnight Mercy nor I own a garter belt."

"Ah, *chère*, I was afraid of that. So I bought one of those too. It's in my back pocket." He turned slightly as he explained, "I couldn't carry everything."

Dangling from the pocket of his jeans was a thin black elastic strip that he hadn't quite managed to shove inside with the rest of the belt. The weight of the hanging clasp caused the garter to sway with his movements, hypnotizing her. She closed her eyes, removing the temptation to linger over Nick's physical attributes, which he made absolutely no attempt to hide.

His jeans weren't actually tight, but they were low slung, a soft well-worn blue, hugging places she'd rather not be caught staring at. His T-shirt could be described as a second skin, and she'd be lying to herself if she denied the instant physical attraction she felt for the man.

Ironically, the garter belt worried her more than the stockings. Never before had a man seen through her so easily. She wasn't the kind of woman who had drawers of sexy lingerie with which she enticed her lovers. Without saying a word, Nick made it very clear that he wanted her and that he knew Midnight Mercy wasn't the real Mercy Malone.

Expelling a heavy breath, she opened her eyes and said, "Damn you. Why can't you be like other men?"

"Don't tell me that men haven't brought you gifts before?"

"Oh, sure." She nodded. "Roses and chocolate. Occasionally Chinese take-out, but never stockings."

"Did you ask them in?"

"No."

"Are you gonna ask me in?" Nick bounced the pink ball once more, teasing the Lab.

"It's either ask you in, or replace the screen when she charges through it to get that damn ball."

"Then I'd have to say I'm glad I'm not like other men."

"You are an original," Mercy allowed as she flipped the screen-door latch and let go of the dog's collar. Immediately, Witch bumped the door frame with her nose, squeezing through the opening. "If I were you, Nick, I'd throw that ball into the yard or prepare to lose your hand."

Instantly, Nick complied, and Witch sailed off the porch, never touching the steps. For the moment

Mercy ignored Nick and watched the fluid motion of her dog as she ran for the rolling tennis ball. At first it looked as if she'd overrun the ball, but in the next second she turned and scooped up the fuzzy pink sphere. Without a wasted motion, she unerringly streaked toward Nick.

"She wants to play, and since you started it, you finish it. By the way, Witch normally won't stop until you've thrown a ball twenty-five times or so. Have fun," Mercy suggested as the dog spit the now soggy ball out on Nick's leather running shoes.

Without a backward glance, Mercy headed for the kitchen. Witch's impatient bark sounded behind her a split second before Nick laughed and said, "Go get it!"

Twenty minutes later she'd made iced tea, cleaned the kitchen, and Nick still hadn't come inside. Giving up, she went back to the front door. Nick and Witch weren't in the front yard. Puzzled, Mercy pushed opened the noisy screen and stepped out onto the large, old-fashioned porch.

"Over here, *chère*," Nick instructed from her left.

He sat in her porch swing, slowly pushing it with one foot as he flicked his gaze over her from top to bottom. Even though only a small portion of stretch leggings extended beyond her oversized T-shirt, Nick still managed to find every curve with his piercing gaze. Since his hands were empty, Mercy could only guess the stockings were safely tucked in the pocket with the garter belt.

"Why are you still out here?" she asked.

"Witch and I were too worn-out to walk all the way across your yard to my car and get my tools."

He didn't look worn-out, but he did look a little sad, like someone who'd been examining old memories. Mercy glanced down at Witch, who lay by the railing, contentedly napping, her muzzle propped on top of the tennis ball. She asked, "What do you need tools for?"

"To fix that screen door. Your dog might be able to sleep through that awful fingernails-on-a-chalkboard noise, but I refuse to listen to the door caterwaul every time I walk through it."

She pointed out, "If I'd wanted my screen door fixed, I could have done it myself."

Nick brushed an imaginary piece of lint off the knee of his jeans. "How's that?"

Irritated, Mercy put her hands on her hips. "Even I can replace a worn-out spring."

"Then why haven't you?"

"Not that it's any of your business, but Ed down at the hardware store didn't have the right size spring. He's got it on special order with his wholesaler."

Sagely, Nick nodded his head. "I bet Ed loves you."

"And why is that?"

"You're a hardware-store owner's dream come true, Mercy. Everything in this house is a special order, and the only thing you know how to do is replace. Trust me, Ed would make a lot less money if you learned how to repair instead of replace. I don't suppose he suggested you buy a small can of spray lubricant and simply oil the spring every once in a while?"

"No," Mercy answered, making a mental note to ask Ed the exact same question.

"I didn't think so," Nick commented as he stopped the swing and stood up. "Like I told you, you need to buy a set of those home-improvement books. I'll get the can out of my toolbox."

Since the solution was so simple, Mercy couldn't refuse without sounding like a complete jerk, but she didn't have to like the fact that she owed Nick another favor. To add to her irritation, Witch leaped up the minute Nick patted his leg. Together they strolled across the yard to the glossy black Chevelle.

Dammit! Not only did Nick like dogs; dogs liked Nick. Babies probably did too.

In no time the door was as good as new. "There you go," Nick said, and handed her the can while he tested the spring one last time. He cocked his head and listened intently as he swung the door back and forth. "No squeaks now."

Mercy shook her head. "Not a one. Thanks for the tip."

"So do you feel grateful enough to actually invite me in?" he asked, although he already had one foot inside the door. "We do need to figure out a theme for this fund-raiser."

Facing him squarely, Mercy said, "I don't know. Are you going to behave?"

Nick laughed and reached out to trace a section of hair that lay against her breast. "I doubt it, but I can try."

By stepping back, Mercy avoided his hand. "Try harder."

"I'm not makin' any promises, *chère*. I warned you before. I'm not near through with you. Especially after that kiss."

"That kiss was a mistake, and you know it! We should both forget it and concentrate on the fund-raiser."

"You gonna stand there and tell me that you can forget a kiss like that?"

"Yes. That's exactly what I'm telling you." Mercy gripped the can so tightly she knew her knuckles had to be white.

"Mercy Malone, you are a very pretty coward and a terrible liar," he whispered softly, and stepped out of her way.

She walked past him, shaking her head. "Heavens, don't you ever stop?"

"Not until I get what I want," he warned as he and Witch followed her in.

Carefully, Mercy set the can on the small half-moon table against the entrance wall. Then she turned around and met his dark gaze, more than a little angry. "And what is it you want? You hint. You insinuate. You tease. But you never play it straight. Exactly what do you want from me, Nick? I don't do one-night stands, and I'm not looking to play house!"

Nick studied her, surprised at the edge in her voice. Not for the first time he wondered what had Mercy running scared. He had a feeling that his being a doctor was only part of it. So he crossed his arms over his chest and said, "Then I guess I'll have to settle for something in between."

"Like what?" Mercy asked, startled by his answer.

"Something like friendship and honesty."

Frustrated, Mercy paced a small circle. "You make it all sound so simple. And it's not." She stopped to stare at him again. "What am I supposed to do with all these confusing feelings?"

"Sort 'em out one at a time, just like everybody does."

Unexpectedly, Mercy's sense of humor surfaced. "And I suppose you're going to do your dead level best to help me sort them out. Aren't you?"

Grinning broadly, Nick admitted, "Now you're talking, *chère*. I thought I might help. What are friends for?"

Mercy groaned. "With friends like you, who needs enemies?"

Nick laughed and then, like a gunfighter disarming himself at the city limits of a "no weapons" town, he pulled the stockings and garter belt from his back pocket and placed them carefully on the table alongside the small spray can. While he held his arms up in surrender he asked, "What does a man have to do to get a drink around here?"

"First you have to promise not to insult the sheriff's iced tea," Mercy told him, hands on her hips.

"Wouldn't dream of it," Nick assured her as he followed her toward the kitchen.

Swirling the melting ice cubes around the bottom of her empty tea glass, Mercy started to make a suggestion and then shook her head without saying anything. They'd been in her office for the better part of an hour trying to come up with a decent title for their fund-raising evening. "Nothing we've come up with is really right. And . . . You're not paying attention again!"

Nick looked up from the pages of one of Mercy's numerous movie-trivia books. The floor-to-ceiling bookshelf behind the desk was filled with star biographies, histories of the "B" and horror movies, trade books on special effects, poster and movie-still photograph collections intended as coffee-table books, three different movie video guides, and the Silver Screen Edition of Trivial Pursuit. "You expect me to pay attention with all of this at my fingertips?"

"Yes, I do."

"All right," Nick said as he closed the book, rested his arms on the desktop, and concentrated on her. She'd claimed a corner of the well-used couch—as far away from him as possible, he noted. "You've got to make up your mind, Mercy. First you chew me out because I pay too much attention, and then you accuse me of paying too little."

"I don't want you to pay attention to me, Nick! I want you to concentrate on the fund-raiser! That *is* what you came here for."

"Is it? I thought I came to fix your screen door and to spend some time with you."

"You thought wrong," Mercy told him bluntly. She sucked on a piece of ice for a moment and then added, "I thought you understood. I don't *spend time* with doctors."

"Not even with your parents?" Nick asked, remembering Sister Agatha's comment about Mercy losing interest in the resident because he'd been like her doctor parents—all medical talk and no action.

"I usually only see them on holidays, birthdays, and, of course, at The Weddings."

Nick could actually hear her capitalize the words.

Intrigued, but knowing better than to betray anything more than a casual interest, he kept his voice carefully neutral as he said, "You make weddings sound like a quirky family tradition."

"Yeah, I guess you could say they are," Mercy acknowledged a tad flippantly. "It's so hard to keep up with who's marrying who that we need scorecards."

"Scorecards?" Nick abandoned his spot behind the desk and took the other corner of the couch.

"All together my parents have been married six times. Only once to each other," Mercy clarified.

Nick lifted a brow. "Six?"

"Well, Mother's engaged again. If she actually marries Vaughn this Thanksgiving, that will make it seven. Of course you can't get married that many times unless you get divorced on a regular basis." Mercy plucked at the arm of the sofa. "What about you, Nick? Are your parents divorced?"

"My parents weren't ever married, *chère*."

"Oh God." Mercy's cheeks turned a fiery red as she apologized. "I'm sorry, Nick."

"Don't be. My mother wasn't. Eventually, she married a man she loved. That's when we moved to Baton Rouge and then to N'Awlins." Nick anchored an ankle over one knee and spread his arms out. "You know, N'Awlins isn't really Cajun country. I always missed the bayou, but Papa Jack was a good man. Raised me like his own."

Mercy wondered at the past tense and the bittersweet tone in his voice. "Is he the one who said precise women spent too much time measuring and not enough enjoying?"

"Yeah. He did. He said a lot of things worth remembering." Not quite sure why, Nick shared something with her that he hadn't told anyone in years. "My parents and my little sister died in a boating accident while I was in medical school."

Mercy closed her eyes and wanted to take back time, wanted to go back to the beginning of this conversation and erase it. She didn't want to feel the compassion she felt for him. She didn't want to know his pain.

I don't have anybody who asks anymore. That's what he'd said when she wanted to know why he hated answering personal questions. How was she ever going to be able to tell the man to go away when he as much as said he didn't have anywhere else to go? She opened her eyes and repeated what seemed to be her own special litany around Nick. "I'm so sorry."

Leaning toward her, Nick took the glass from her hand. "It's okay, *chère*. I wanted you to know. It was a long time ago. I've learned to live with it." Slapping one jean-sheathed thigh, he banished the sadness he knew was in his eyes and got up. "Look, you want to get something to eat? I'm starved."

Mercy checked the clock on her desk. Almost six o'clock. "Maybe a rain check? I've got to finish viewing next week's movie and get started on my comments for the show. I usually do that on Sunday afternoons."

"Fine." Nick started to walk away. "You finish that, and I'll cook."

"No!" The abrupt denial stopped him on his way out the door. Mercy felt like a heel, but the last thing she needed was to let Nick keep helping and fixing.

Ignoring her feelings for him would only become more difficult with every confidence and intimacy they shared. As he looked over his shoulder she offered the first excuse she could think of, "I haven't been to the grocery this week. There's nothing here."

With a laugh, Nick waved aside her concerns. "Then it's gonna have to be gumbo."

"I hope you have the recipe memorized, because I don't have a cookbook."

"Darlin', gumbo's not a recipe. It's a scavenger hunt."

"I'm telling you. You're not going to find anything fit to eat in my refrigerator."

"Well, you relax and let me be the judge of that."

"You can't possibly know how to make gumbo. You're a man," Mercy said as if that would settle everything.

"The secret to gumbo and every other Cajun dish is—first, you make a roux. Anybody born in South Lou'siana can make a roux. All you need is a little butter and a little flour. Are you gonna tell me your cupboard's so bare that you haven't got butter and flour?"

"Gumbo's a little more complicated than that."

"Not really. I don't know how you do it here, but in Lou'siana, we bring everything to a boil, and then cut back the heat." A glint in his eyes and the husky tone of his voice warned Mercy that he wasn't talking about cooking anymore. "We let it simmer real slow. Until your mouth waters every time you take a breath. Until the only thing on your mind is tasting what you've been waiting for."

Mercy managed to force out an answer, but the words stumbled over one another in a nervous rush, betraying the effect Nick's words had on her. "I guess you do know what you're doing."

"That"—Nick gave her a wink as he walked out of the room—"I guaran-damn-tee."

With one hand Mercy reached for the VCR control. With the other she rubbed her chest as if that would stop the thumping of her heart and the racing of her pulse.

SIX

Pleased that he'd overcome Mercy's objections to sharing dinner, Nick thumbed on the radio in her kitchen and got to work by inspecting the contents of the refrigerator. He discovered that Mercy truly hadn't been to the grocery store. There wasn't *much* of anything, but there was a *little* of everything. And that was all right. A little of everything would make a wonderful gumbo.

As a flour-and-butter mixture bubbled in an electric skillet, he began piling an odd assortment of ingredients on the counter to wait their turn: a couple of foil-wrapped, leftover chicken breasts, a package of frozen okra, a couple of tomatoes, Polish sausage, Worcestershire sauce, and Tabasco sauce. In another frying pan he began sautéing a yellow onion, celery that had seen better days, and half of a red bell pepper he found in a plastic sandwich bag. He hadn't been especially neat with the chopping, but then gumbo didn't require painstaking preparation.

A traditional gumbo just required a big pot and time to simmer.

Time to simmer was just what Mercy needed too, he thought. Romancing her was turning out to be a lot like Cajun cooking, and he silently thanked his mother for drumming the basic concepts—of Cajun cuisine, and of life—into his head. Never rush a roux. Never rush a woman.

He kept her advice in mind as he stirred the bubbling roux, making sure it didn't burn. A roux had to "earn" its brown color slowly. Then he had to add water and put everything in a pot to simmer for an hour.

Since he didn't intend to rush his roux or Mercy Malone, Nick figured the gumbo wouldn't be ready until she'd had enough time to watch her movie and finish her work. Once they sat down to dinner, she'd have no excuses. The rest of her evening belonged to him. Whistling, he reached for the broiled chicken and began pulling meat off the bone.

By seven-thirty, Mercy's stomach began to grumble, encouraged by an incredible aroma that had begun as faint cooking smells and had now coalesced into a delicious promise that filled the house. She pulled her glasses off and rubbed her eyes. Nick was fighting dirty, hitting her right in her lumberjack appetite. For a few more minutes she uselessly shuffled her notes and then gave up.

Honesty compelled her to admit that the desire to be in the same room with Nick's potent sexuality was as real as the desire to assuage her hunger. Both cravings, in equal measure, sent her downstairs. She suspected that the adrenaline surge she got every time Nick looked at her might be addictive. It was as if her brain and body clicked into high gear anytime he walked into a room.

As she trailed downstairs she wondered when she had abandoned her carefully cultivated principles for a safe, happy life. Number one: Avoid attraction because it leads to lust, which leads to love, which leads to bitterness and ugliness. Number two: Don't let a man get comfortable in your house, because that's only a step away from letting him into your life. Number three: Never trust your heart to a doctor because doctors care more about medicine than about people and relationships.

Mercy pushed open the door into the kitchen and admitted that if she hadn't ignored the first two rules the moment she saw Nick Devereaux standing on her porch, he wouldn't be worming his way into her life right now. Thank God for rule number three. If it weren't for that, she'd be headed for real trouble. After seeing him in the emergency room, she shouldn't have any trouble remembering that he was a doctor.

Turned away from her, Nick stood in the open doorway across the room, shoulder propped against the back doorjamb and staring out into the yard. Everything about him was a contradiction. He was tough and gentle. Dangerous and safe. Rough and smooth. More than anything else, she knew he was alone, and she *hated* knowing that. The first night he walked into her house, she'd jokingly told Joan that she was a sucker for a good cause.

Right now she didn't want to be a sucker. She'd give anything if Nick hadn't told her about the death of his family. If he hadn't pretended he was okay because the passage of time had erased his hurt. If she hadn't seen that world-weary look in his eyes when he sat at her kitchen table, eating pizza and thumbing the label of his beer bottle.

Mercy knew she was in trouble, because she wanted to be Nick's friend. He needed one. And she didn't know if she could do that without the chemistry getting in the way. Nick had made it very plain that the only thing standing between them and a nice soft bed was time and her resistance.

Friends spent *time* together. How long could she resist the sexual pull between them when friendship made her want to put her arms around him and show him he wasn't alone?

"You going to stare at my butt all night?" Nick asked without turning around.

Startled out of her thoughts, Mercy defended herself. "I was *not* staring at your butt!"

Nick turned around slowly, making her pulse jump when his gaze wound its way up her body and rested on her mouth. He had a way of looking at her that she was beginning to recognize as his way of making love without touching. Finally, Nick said, "Not the buns? Guess you're a leg woman."

"Shoulders. I like very broad shoulders," Mercy corrected, well aware that Nick had maneuvered the conversation toward the physical attraction between them.

His laughter left no doubt that he took great pleasure in stirring up her sexual awareness. It seemed to be his purpose in life. Unfortunately, she'd begun to like matching wits with him. She liked the way he challenged her with words, daring her to top him, laughing when she did, and backing off until the next time.

Suddenly she realized that their verbal dance was what flirting was meant to be—not that insufferably cute chatter exchanged at cocktail parties, but an exchange of words that promised everything sensual and forced nothing. Flirting, in the hands of someone dedicated like Nick, was extended foreplay. Dear God! And she wanted to be Nick's friend?

"Broad enough for you?" Nick asked, obviously unconcerned about whether his shoulders would make the grade. When he crossed his arms, his T-shirt barely covered the waistband of his jeans. Another half inch and skin would be showing.

Mercy eyed the edge of his shirt for a moment as Nick shifted and then said, "You'll do."

"Good. But you and I both know the real test is whether or not I can make gumbo. The only direct route to Mercy Malone's heart is straight through her stomach."

"Sad, but true," Mercy agreed, glad the conversation was back in safe territory. She made a beeline for the stove and pulled the lid off the pot. "I cannot believe you found anything in my kitchen that could produce something that smells this heavenly!"

"Oh, ye of little faith," Nick accused. "Sister Agatha told me that you were long on doubt and short on faith . . . where men were concerned. I'll have to see what I can do about changin' that."

"Sister Agatha told you that about me?" she questioned sharply.

"Yeah."

Mercy was more convinced than ever that the nun was subtly egging Nick on, offering him a challenge, making sure he stayed interested. Worried, she reached for the large spoon beside the pot as she asked, "What else has she told you?"

"That you always had a good heart even if you kept it on a short leash."

Embarrassed by the unexpected compliment, Mercy stirred the thick, fragrant mixture and inhaled deeply before she answered. "I wouldn't believe everything Sister tells you. She won't be happy until every single person she knows is married with children."

Nick opened a couple of cabinets, looking for bowls, as he asked, "Is that your way of telling me you don't believe in marriage, or kids, or both?"

"Marriage and children are just fine as long—" Mercy stopped abruptly, biting her lip. Somehow she always said too much in front of Nick.

"As long as you're not the one with the husband, and the kids aren't yours," he finished for her, and slowly retrieved two bowls before turning around.

Meeting his gaze squarely, Mercy denied his interpretation. "I didn't say that."

"But I did. You're a pretty hard case, *chère*. You've got a lot of rules—no doctors, no marrying men, no children. I'm sorry, but I just don't buy it. You've already got the house and the white picket fence."

"I'm not asking you to buy anything!"

"Does that mean you do think about marriage and kids?"

"Are you sure you went to medical school and not to law school? Let it go, Nick. I'm not going to let you twist me up and confuse me. All I said was that Sister Agatha had marriage on her mind." Mercy gave the gumbo a good hard stir. Marriage was the problem, not children. "I will admit, however, that you can raid my kitchen anytime if the result tastes half as good as this concoction smells."

"Does that mean you're hungry?" Nick took the spoon from her.

"Do alligators live in the bayou?" Mercy asked sarcastically as he spooned rice from another pan into their dishes.

"Indeed they do, darlin'. And you'd best be nice to this 'gator or he'll take a bite of you to keep for himself. Now go sit down."

"Gladly!" Mercy took a seat at the oak table and waited for Nick to scoop up dinner. She didn't mind Nick tossing out orders as long as he stopped asking questions. Of course, she thought, she could always start asking a few. "Is this domestic demonstration for my benefit or do you actually cook for yourself?"

"I'm more of a microwave gourmet," he confessed as he ladled gumbo over the rice in her bowl.

"You can make a supper like this appear out of thin air, and you don't cook much?" Mercy asked as she accepted the steaming gumbo. "That's a shame. Don't you know that a great cook is a terrible thing to waste!"

Nick licked a spot of rich Cajun stew off his thumb. "Cooking for one isn't nearly as much fun as cooking for a crowd."

"Why's that?" Mercy pretended not to notice the way his tongue laved the side of his thumb.

"No applause when you're finished," he joked, and then gave her a half smile. "I'd rather nuke a frozen dinner and toss the tray when I'm done. Besides, setting and clearing off a table for one seems so sad."

Silently, Mercy agreed and ignored the little twinge in the area of her heart. Aloud, she asked, "Did you cook much in New Orleans?"

Nick returned to the stove and served his gumbo before he said, "Mercy, if you want to know if I walked away from a relationship back in N'Awlins, all you have to do is ask."

Mercy, who'd been about to take her first bite, put the spoon back down. "Your ego is incredible. I wasn't asking about your past relationships! I just thought you might have had more friends in New Orleans. More occasions to cook for people."

"Cook for a woman, you mean." Nick settled himself across the table and held out a paper towel for her to use as a napkin. "And the answer to all your questions, spoken and unspoken, is no. I didn't cook romantic candlelit dinners in N'Awlins. I didn't much feel like it before, but I may give it a try now."

He waved the towel slightly since she seemed to have stopped in the middle of reaching for it. "I've never been married, and I didn't move to Louisville to get away from a bad relationship."

Pulling the towel from his grasp, Mercy said, "I wasn't going to ask any of those questions!" She paused and worried her lip with her teeth. "But since you've brought it up yourself, don't expect me to believe you've been leading the life of a monk!"

"I didn't say I was celibate," Nick pointed out. "I just wasn't involved with anyone on a steady basis. I wasn't much of a long-term bargain in those days."

The first to look away, Mercy chastised herself for letting his confession get to her. Only a sucker would want to ask questions or delve into his past. She sternly reminded herself that she didn't want to know anything else about the man. Besides, she didn't need to ask why he hadn't been "much of a bargain."

Nick Devereaux was a doctor, and that was all the explanation she needed. Living with doctors had taught her a lot about long hours, emotional on-and-off switches, preoccupation with patients, canceled vacations, and beepers going off. While she could admire and even understand her parents' commitment to medicine, she couldn't understand how their careers made up for all the lost happiness in their lives.

If you know so much about doctors. then why does Nick seem to have plenty of time on his hands? Time he appears to be happy to spend with you?

Unable to answer that question and determined to maintain some distance, she dug into the gumbo with a vengeance. One bite and flavor exploded in her mouth. She closed her eyes to savor the experience. "Mmm. This is heaven."

"Not quite, *chère*," Nick pronounced after he'd tasted the gumbo with the same intensity of a wine connoisseur sampling a fine vintage. "This is adequate, but not spectacular."

"I disagree," Mercy told him as she took another quick bite. "You could not improve on this."

"A clove of garlic would have been nice."

Mercy shuddered. "Garlic? In this house? Perish the thought. Think of my reputation! Vampires around the world would never speak to me again."

Smacking his forehead with the palm of one hand, Nick apologized, "How foolish of me not to have realized."

"Don't mention silver bullets around here either," Mercy lectured him with a grin that ruined the effect.

"Yes, ma'am. I forgot for a moment that this is Haunt, Kentucky. I assume every house has a ghost?"

"Every one but mine."

"What? No ghosts!"

"Ghosts cost extra," Mercy explained as she wiped the corner of her mouth. "I could barely afford Haunt's Creaky Noise Package." After pausing to take a bite, she continued, "Local television personalities are not rolling in dough like most people think. When I bought this place, I had to give up expensive restaurants, vacations that involved airplanes, and my apartment in the city."

"Are you sorry?"

"Absolutely not." Mercy shook her head for emphasis. "Not many towns have an atmosphere like Haunt, Kentucky."

Nick shook his head. "Halloween around this place must be a regular ghouls' night out."

Dropping her spoon, Mercy cried, "That's it!"

"That's what?"

"Ghouls' Nite Out. That's the benefit." Mercy doubled her fist and pounded the table. "That's our theme!"

Nick enjoyed the animation in her face. In fact, he'd enjoyed the change in Mercy since she'd come downstairs. She seemed more at ease with him, more willing to let down her guard and treat him like a friend instead of a dangerous adversary. He wasn't sure what had caused the change, but he enjoyed it.

"Well, say *something*!" she ordered as she scraped a bite of gumbo from the bottom of her bowl.

"I think it's a great idea."

"We can promote it as an evening of black ties and black stalkings." Mercy spread the fingers on her hand and swept it through the air as though envisioning a theater marquee.

Laughing out loud, Nick pushed his chair back from the table. "*Dieu!* But you're quick! Does everything always fall so easily into place for you?"

Self-conscious, Mercy took a swig of iced tea before she answered. "Things like this? Yeah, but usually I have to wait two beats for someone to get the joke, or even worse, explain it to them." She looked at him thoughtfully. "Except with you."

"Same wavelength."

"That's a scary thought!" Mercy laughed, but groaned inwardly. Sharing a sense of humor with Nick was one more crack in the invisible wall that kept her from crossing the line between friendship and relationship. The last thing she needed was another crack in her wall. Since Nick arrived on her doorstep and pulled off his sunglasses, the damn thing was crumbling faster than she could repair it.

"More gumbo?" Nick asked as he got up to take his bowl to the sink.

Mercy hesitated. "First tell me if it's still going to taste this good if I warm up some later."

"Even better," Nick promised.

"Then I can wait."

"Patience. Another trait we share," Nick commented as he held out his hand for her bowl. When Mercy gave it to him, she made very sure their hands didn't touch. Nick kept his next suggestion very innocent, hoping she wouldn't instantly recognize it as a ploy to delay his departure. Which of course it was. "What do you say to setting this pot of gumbo in the refrigerator and taking a walk? We can brainstorm about the benefit some more."

As soon as he said "walk," Witch materialized from under the table. Her front feet did a Gene Kelly tap dance on the checkerboard linoleum.

"Is this like the tennis ball thing?" Nick asked dryly.

"Yeah." Mercy nodded as Witch spun in a tiny circle. "You said the magic word and now one of us is going to have to go around the block." Her expression made it clear exactly which one of them would be going.

"I'm scared of the dark," Nick lied as he met her amused gaze. "Someone will have to come with me for protection."

Mercy got Witch's leash from a hook in the pantry and handed it to him as she said, "You don't look like you need protection, and you don't look scared. Besides, you'll have Witch with you."

"Oh, but you're wrong, *chère*. Sophie Jensen scares the hell out of me, and I don't think Witch is gonna be much help."

Cringing at the images that sprang to mind, Mercy agreed, "All right. I'll come with you. God only knows what scheme you and Sophie would come up with if I left you alone."

The twilight ebbed into night as they made their second journey around the block. They trailed behind Witch, who drifted along in a zigzag pattern, investigating each edge of the sidewalk. Simultaneously, porch lights and night stars winked on. Nick listened to the familiar cadence created by the opening and shutting of doors, barking dogs, children's laughter, and a father's shouted reminder that it was time to come in.

All around him was the sound of community, something he hadn't even realized he missed. Children's laughter was one sound he had avoided at all costs since the accident. It reminded him of his sister, Catherine. She had rarely laughed, but when she did, she laughed with such joy and abandon that one by one the rest of the family joined in. Sometimes without ever knowing why, or caring.

Most children acquired nicknames early in life, but his little sister had been Catherine since the day she was born. It fit her the way a *'tit nom* never could. He'd been fifteen years old when she was born, and he remembered it like it was yesterday. He remembered pretending to be too cool to fuss over a baby, and then talking nonsense to her when no one else was in the room.

From the time she could walk, she'd followed him around like a gentle puppy. No one ever doubted how she felt about her big brother. No one had been prouder than Catherine that he was going to be a doctor. He missed her. He missed his parents, but losing Catherine had been like losing a child.

He'd been able to put aside the memories during medical school, internship, and residency. The incredible work load had been a blessing, but eventually he'd had to face the real world again. Four years ago, he'd forced himself to go back to New Orleans, and then the insomnia started. He couldn't deal with the memories. So he withdrew, creating a safe, sterile existence without nosy neighbors, close friends, or laughing children. And the silence woke him up at night.

Nothing surprised him more than to hear the noises of Haunt, Kentucky, and realize he wanted noise back in his life.

"I could learn to like this place," he said, shortening his steps to match Mercy's slower pace.

Mercy pulled in a deep breath of summer air, warm and ripe. "Hmm, I know what you mean. I fell in love with this place the moment I saw it. Narrow streets, big trees."

"Sounds like the perfect place to put down roots."

"It has been."

"Must not be very strong roots. You're already planning to move to Pittsburgh."

"Who said I was?"

"You did," Nick reminded her.

"Oh, that. That was *career* talk." Mercy rubbed her arms and gave a deep sigh. "I'll go if Dan pushes me to it, but I don't think he wants me to go any more than I want to go. I suspect we'll come to an agreement of some sort. Right now we're only circling each other, getting ready for the big negotiation."

Startled, Nick looked at her long and hard. "Excuse me, but I thought *career* opportunities this good were few and far between. You're telling me that you're gonna pass up a chance at the big time to stay in Louisville?"

"Sure. If it doesn't work out, I can always go to medical school." Mercy's grin teased him.

"Oh, I got a picture of that, *chère*!"

"Okay, so maybe I wouldn't. I sure didn't like it the first time."

Nick stopped dead in his tracks and stared. Witch ran out of slack and turned to investigate why her leash had grown suddenly short.

"Yeah, you heard me right." Mercy grabbed his arm and pulled him along. "I didn't actually make it to medical school. I jumped ship my sophomore year of college and switched all my premed classes to journalism and communications."

"Too bad. You'd have made a wonderful doctor," Nick told her as they waited for one of Mercy's neighbors to back out of the driveway. Nick waved right along with Mercy as he said, "I can see you in family practice or maybe pediatrics. You have a way with people. I saw it when you put that orderly at ease and when we toured the ER."

"Well, all my parents could see was a surgical residency. Dad was really leaning on me to persue neurosurgery, but Mother had pretty much decided on my being a heart surgeon," Mercy said when they started walking again.

"What changed your mind? Couldn't be the blood and guts. You'll see more of that watching horror films than you'd ever see in an operating room."

"Funny."

"Thank you." Nick grinned. "Come on, Mercy. Why did you back out?"

For some reason, Nick's word choices were beginning to bother her. Mercy reached to unsnap Witch's collar as they walked into the yard. "I didn't back out. I changed my mind."

"Why?"

"For lots of reasons."

"Like what?"

A little exasperated, she said, "You don't want to listen to old history."

"It beats goin' home and staring at the ceiling," Nick informed her as he took her hand and led her up the steps. "Insomnia and I are old friends. You wouldn't want to be responsible for another sleepless night?"

"No," Mercy answered faintly, climbing the steps, her attention focused on the warmth of his hand clasping hers. Friends hold hands, she told herself. His touch meant nothing. The tingling meant nothing. The tiny charge of electricity could be explained by the laws of everyday, ordinary physics or chemistry or something. Just like the shock people got from walking across a carpet and touching something metal.

Then why did holding his hand feel like a dangerous thing to do?

The abrupt halt of their progress brought her attention back to the real world. She noticed two things immediately: One, she hadn't turned on the porch light before they left the house, and two, Nick clearly waited for a response to something he'd said. Since she hadn't heard a word out of the last dozen or so, she had to ask. "What?"

"I said—" Pleased, Nick saw the way her eyes kept straying toward their entwined fingers, which meant she must have noticed the perfect fit. He settled himself on the wooden swing without letting go of her hand and then pulled her onto the seat beside him. He would rather have pulled her into his lap, but he didn't want to jeopardize the progress he'd made tonight. "I said that I'd much rather sit in this old-fashioned swing and listen to ancient history than go home. There's nothing there anymore except designer cobwebs."

Carefully, he pushed against the porch with his foot, gently rocking the swing. As the air swirled around them, the scent of the potted nicotiana set along the railing teased his senses. The faint glow of the streetlight illuminated Witch as she found a spot by the screen door and curled up. Nick smiled to himself as Mercy relaxed enough to let her thigh touch his. "You gonna tell me about your brush with medical school or am I gonna have to drag every detail out of you?"

Mercy self-consciously disengaged her hand from his, which rested much too intimately on his leg. "There aren't any details. It's not much of a story, really. I had an incredibly shy college roommate who was in love, from afar of course, with one of the graduate assistants in the journalism department. So she talked me into taking this television news lab that was offered as an elective for nonmajors. She needed moral support since the grad assistant was teaching the class. One thing led to another, and suddenly I was having to explain to my folks why I dropped out of the premed curriculum."

She shrugged to signal the end of the story. "When I got out of college, I snagged a job doing a midnight recap of the news before the movie came on. I love movies, and the rest, as they say, is history."

"That's it?" Nick chided in disappointment. He adjusted his body and ran his arm along the back of the swing as he leaned toward Mercy, not coincidentally pressing his thigh more intimately against hers. "Aren't you leaving something out?"

"I don't think so." Warily, Mercy stiffened. "I told you it wasn't much of a story."

"But what about the roommate? Did love conquer all?"

"Oh, her!" Stifling a giggle, Mercy relaxed against his arm. "Turns out the grad assistant was married and a very proud papa, who'd lost his wedding ring down the kitchen sink. My roommate dropped the course after the second class."

"How many classes did it take before you realized you wanted this career more than medicine?"

"Oh, I never wanted to be a doctor. That's what my parents wanted for me. You know how everybody asks you what you want to be when you grow up?"

"Yeah."

"Well, in my house, it was never a question. It was a statement. You know: 'This is our daughter. Mercy wants to be a surgeon.' How about you? When did you decide to become a doctor?"

Nick slowed the swing's motion to a gentle sway. "I was young. I think I was ten. Ten or eleven. Hell, I don't remember, it's been so long." He laughed softly and shook his head as if surprised by how much time had passed. "I was a kid, playing where I shouldn't have been, and cut my leg." He drew a line on his thigh. "Twenty-four stitches. I remember watching the doctor magically close up that wound. I remember thinking that sewing up people was the coolest job in the world."

"And that's when you decided on emergency medicine," Mercy guessed immediately.

"No, not then."

"Then why did you pick the ER?"

Nick didn't want to lie to Mercy, but he wasn't about to tell her the real reason he chose emergency medicine either. Even in his own mind the reason often sounded like a gutless cop-out, so he gave her the same glib answer he gave everyone. "I fell in love with emergency medicine the instant I found out that ER schedules are flexible. Of course, the bad news is that I don't make the kind of cash I would have made if I'd gone into the big-money specialties. Especially at Mercy Hospital."

Although she'd been around hospitals most of her life, Mercy hadn't paid much attention to emergency departments. In her mind, a spade was a spade and a doctor was a doctor. "What do you mean flexible schedules?"

"I work a bunch of long days and then get a chunk of time off."

"How many days and how big a chunk?"

"I work a seven-A.M.-to-seven-P.M. shift one week, and the next week I'm off."

"A whole week off?"

"Yeah. Free-as-a-bird."

"Except for your beeper."

"I don't carry a beeper, *chère*. You can frisk me if you want," he offered. The swing wobbled a little as he spread his arms.

"Every doctor carries a beeper or one of those cellular phones. The AMA made an amendment to the Hippocratic oath or something. How else is the service going to get a hold of you?"

"They don't need to. And I don't carry a beeper," he repeated. "Neither do the other ER doctors at Mercy Hospital."

"God forbid they should need you in an emergency."

"The nurses know how to dial a phone, *chère*. I keep telling you, but you don't seem to understand. Mercy Hospital is a small, community hospital, not a trauma center. If the nurses need us after seven at night, they just start calling. But unless they're expecting multiple cases from a bar brawl, or a building collapses, they don't call us. They call the patient's doctor. Sometimes the patient's already called his doctor before he shows up. Most people would rather have an orthopedic specialist set their leg or a plastic surgeon sew up their face."

"Yeah, that makes sense," Mercy admitted. "But what good is an emergency room without doctors? Patients could bleed to death waiting for one of you guys to answer the phone!"

"That's what big trauma centers are for. The paramedics will get the patient where he needs to be. I'd love to see Mercy Hospital staffed twenty-four hours a day, but none of the small emergency departments can afford that. We only have a couple of residents covering the whole hospital at night. You saw our facility."

"Yeah." Mercy remembered all the broken tiles, the barren lounge, the dungeonlike atmosphere. "No money."

"Since I got here, we're working a twelve-to-twelve shift on Fridays instead of a seven to seven. In fact, the other doctors are complaining that it's turning into our busiest night." Nick grinned. "You'd think we were running two-for-one specials or offering a free gift with purchase."

That drew a small, pained laugh out of Mercy. "You make it sound like working at the cosmetic counter of a department store."

"There are similarities. People step up to the counter looking for miracles. Sometimes we don't have 'em."

"Is that what you hate most? Losing?"

"Among other things," Nick evaded smoothly.

"Like what?"

"Disarming the patients."

"What?" Mercy thought maybe she hadn't heard him correctly.

"Disarming the patients. It's an inner-city hospital, Mercy. Our client base isn't only poor families. We also provide care to the drug addicts, the dealers, and the gangs. I've taken knives off them. Guns. Whatever. And it's not just the patients. Their buddies that bring them in are armed too."

Mercy shuddered. "Ever think about changing specialties? Or going into family practice?"

"Nope," he answered without hesitation. Family practice with its intimate, long-term patient care was out of the question, and once he made up his mind, he rarely changed it. Pursuing Mercy was the one exception in recent memory. When he left New Orleans, he'd made up his mind that he was better off alone, starting over well away from the reminders of a different time. That is, until he met Mercy. In a heartbeat, she changed his mind about being alone. Now all he had to do was change hers.

Reminded of the real reason for his visit today, Nick decided it was time to put his cards on the table. Papa Jack always told him it never hurt to ask. "You ever thought about giving a doctor the benefit of the doubt?"

"How do you mean?" Mercy countered uneasily.

"If I remember correctly, Sister Agatha said your opinion of doctors is that they're all medical talk and no action. I'd like to prove you wrong." Nick wove his fingers into the hair that hung down her back, slipping through the russet curtain and testing the satiny skin at the nape of her neck. Lowering his voice, he added, "If you'll give me the chance."

Mercy shivered at the first contact, melted when his expert fingers began to massage the muscles of her neck, and felt the vibration of the earthy tone of his voice all the way down to her toes. "You said you'd behave."

"I said I'd try."

"What happened to friendship and honesty?" She forced herself to stand up and move away from his touch.

"They're still here, *chère*," Nick assured her softly as he followed her, taking her arm and turning her.

"They're not gonna go away just 'cause I want more." When she didn't pull away, Nick cupped her head with his hands and urged her to look into his eyes. "Good or bad, there is something going on between the two of us."

Mercy couldn't deny that any more than she could deny the racing of her heart. She could only tell him the truth. "But I don't want there to be."

"Aw, darlin', you can't hide your head in the sand and pretend we don't strike sparks off each other."

"Why not?" It sounded like the perfection solution to her.

"Because I won't let you."

"That's not fair," she whispered.

"I don't care," he told her as he widened his stance and leaned against the house. Nick dropped his arms to her waist and pulled her into the spot created by his parted thighs. "It's been a long time since I wanted anything, and I'm not going to let you hide from this."

"But what do you really want from me, Nick?"

"I don't know, *chère*. I don't know. Maybe just a little time to figure it out. Maybe just a place to be that feels right."

Nick's simple human need to connect with another person tugged at her emotions. Mercy drew her breath in sharply when Nick's hands shifted again. This time to her hips, bringing her all the way in, refusing to let her maintain even the smallest distance from the heat of his body. Her hands rested on the soft cotton of his black T-shirt, and her traitorous fingers itched to explore the contours beneath them.

Get a grip, Mercy May, she ordered, and focused her gaze on the topaz ring she wore. She couldn't risk looking at Nick.

Given an inch, Nick Devereaux would take a mile. Maybe that's what scared her about him. He never gave her time to adjust to one level of their relationship before he began the assault on the next plateau. And her body was on his side! It was like fighting two enemies at the same time. She understood how the Mummy must have felt when faced with both Abbott and Costello.

"You feel good here, *chère*." His palms rubbed slow circles high on her hips, rocking her and pressing her against his erection. His dark eyes caught and held hers. "Kinda like you were made for this spot. And you're gonna go and tell me that I should ignore this? I don't think that's right."

A soft groan slipped out of Mercy as her body wrenched the reins of control from her and responded to Nick's suggestive motions with a nudge of its own. "We can't afford this kind of tension if we're going to work together."

"Then, as your doctor, I'd have to recommend you relieve that tension."

SEVEN

This time Nick didn't wait for Mercy to come to him. He took the kiss he wanted. Her lips beneath his were warm and responsive as he ran his tongue between them, teasing past the barrier of her teeth as he slid into the welcoming velvet of her mouth. He groaned at the sensations created by the thrust and parry of their tongues. His hands found her arms, and he moved them up to circle his neck, reveling in his victory when she wove her fingers into his hair.

Nick pulled back slightly, letting their tongues mate in the air before sealing his lips to hers again. He couldn't get enough of her, needed to touch her everywhere at once. His hands bracketed her sides beneath her shirt, and his thumbs rubbed rhythmically up and down her rib cage, coming closer to the sweet fullness of her breasts each time.

When he finally swept his thumbs against the swell of tender flesh, Mercy made a low, soft noise in the back of her throat, which generated an instant response from his already hard body. One quiet signal of pleasure created an intense desire to hear that sound again and again. And he had no intention of being denied. Slowly, he caressed the small of her back with one hand and continued to tease her breast with the other. The textures of smooth skin, satin, lace, and the nub of her aroused nipple had him hot as hell as he smoothed his fingers over the lush landscape of her body.

When he felt her push her breast into his hand, he broke the kiss and let his lips slide down the column of her neck. Mercy wanted him as much as he wanted her. Regardless of her staunch determination to draw the line at friendship, right now she wanted the same things he did. Instinctively, he pressed his arousal against her belly in cadence with the pulsing blood that fired his passion.

Mercy barely could think by the time Nick had pulled his lips away from her mouth, but that had been no respite. He merely began an assault on the hollow at the base of her throat. His mouth teased her with a preview of what his lips and tongue would feel like against her nipples. His fingers created incredible sensations in her breasts that were echoed at the apex of her thighs.

She wanted him. Right or wrong, this hunger needed to be sated. For once, the future and the past were forgotten, because the present was so much more important and common sense eluded her.

If all hell hadn't suddenly erupted behind them, Mercy would never have stopped what was happening between them. But all hell did erupt. Witch growled deep in her throat, and then everything happened at the speed of light. As the Lab sprang to attack an unknown enemy, her compact body collided with Mercy's already rubbery legs and sent her reeling. Nick's back thudded heavily against the house siding as he struggled to steady himself.

Both of them watched in stunned shock as Witch leaped onto the swing, scrambling for balance, and then lunged at a shadow between the potted flowers as the swing neared the porch railing. The hiss of a surprised wild animal was unmistakable, and Mercy's gorgeous pots of blooming flowers started plummeting to the ground when the animal sent them flying as it fled from the dog.

Witch would have jumped the railing and followed if Nick's deadly serious command hadn't forced her to halt. "No! Get back!"

The dog teetered in the swing for a moment, barking and looking longingly toward the side of the house. Witch was clearly torn between obedience and instinct. Eventually, she hopped off the swing, but she continued to pace back and forth across the porch beneath Nick's watchful eye.

Mercy wanted to believe that the shaky feeling inside her bones was a direct result of Witch's having scared the daylights out of her, but she knew the shakes were from coming so close to making a very big and very irreversible mistake with Nick. A mistake she'd sworn not four hours ago to avoid. Careful to keep her distance, she surveyed the damage. In an unsteady voice, she asked, "What was that all about?"

"Well, *chère*, unless you've got an awfully big, silver, striped-tail, pointy-faced, black-masked cat in the neighborhood, I think you had a *chaoui* come callin'."

"A raccoon?"

Turning to look at her, Nick said, "Yeah. And as far as I'm concerned, he couldn't have picked a worse time." He leaned back against the wall, drawing one knee up and resting the flat of his foot against the side of the house. When she started to inspect the broken shards of red clay pots, Nick said, "That mess will wait. I won't. Come here."

"I don't think so."

"Non? Mais yeah, chère. Viens ici," he ordered again, and waited for her to come to him.

With a shake of her head, Mercy took a step backward, putting more distance between herself and the man who seduced her with words she couldn't translate but understood completely. However, understanding what he wanted didn't mean she had any intention of complying. Not now. Barking dogs and shattered pots had broken the spell and reawakened her common sense. "Look, that kiss was a bad idea. It's only going to get in the way of our working together. I don't know what I was thinking before when—"

"If you could still think, then I wasn't doing it right," Nick said, and straightened, more than willing to give kissing another try.

"Dammit, Nick! Stay over there!" Her eyes sought his in the darkness, and he stopped. "We need to talk."

"I'm all talked out."

"But I'm not," Mercy told him sharply. "And this time I want you to listen to what I'm trying to tell you."

Without another word, Nick acquiesced to her demand, holding his arms extended, palms out. Then he dusted potting soil off the white porch swing and sat down. "So . . . talk to me."

Mercy huffed disgustedly and paced in a tiny circle. *So . . . talk to me.* He managed to make even those innocuous little words sound like pillow talk. Face it, Mercy May, she told herself, the problem isn't Nick. The problem was her reaction to him, and it scared the hell out of her. He was the first man she couldn't put out of her mind the moment he left a room.

Life had been so much easier when she'd been the one doing the picking and the choosing instead of the one doing the wanting. In her mind, admitting that she wanted Nick was tantamount to accepting that she'd eventually turn into one of the walking wounded. Just like her parents.

Both her parents bled when relationships ended. Her father stopped the bleeding with alcohol while her mother believed in starving a cold and feeding a depression. Mercy didn't want that for herself. And she didn't want Nick to sell her a ticket for a roller coaster of emotional binging. She wasn't sure she could turn her emotions on and off the way Nick had learned to do as an ER doctor.

Leaning against the porch railing, Mercy chewed her bottom lip, well aware that Nick would continue to wait, wearing that innocent expression, until she spit out what she wanted to say. When she couldn't stand the silence any longer, she plunged. "What happened here . . . when we . . . that kiss tonight wasn't real."

Nick's derisive snort succinctly expressed his opinion about that statement. "That's about as real as it gets. Except maybe for that first one in the hospital."

"Neither of them was a *kiss* kiss. We just got carried away. Think about this clearly. Our first kiss was a childish dare! You called me a coward, and this kiss was simply a culturally conditioned response." Mercy put everything she had into convincing him that they'd stumbled into two meaningless kisses.

"Come on, Nick. Admit it. You were pushing my buttons the first time, and tonight . . . well, look around you! The stars are out; it's a pretty night. You're lonely; you said so yourself. We exchanged a few confidences, got chummy. We'd been sitting in a romantic swing for Pete's sake!"

"Romantic? I don't think so. Maybe I should refresh your memory, *chère*." Slowly, very deliberately, Nick leaned forward, resting his elbows on wide-spread thighs. "Romantic implies hearts and flowers. You and I . . . we're all birds and bees. Now, I'll buy hot as an adjective, but not romantic. We were standing over there. You were between my thighs. We were belly to belly, and my hands were—"

"I know exactly where your hands were!" she snapped.

A smile broke across Nick's face. "Good. I got that right at least."

"Witch, lie down!" Mercy ordered crossly when she couldn't think of a suitable reply, much less deny that Nick was—as Sophie put it—good with his hands. After the dog stopped pacing and sank unhappily down, Mercy felt a pinch of guilt for taking her frustration out on her dog. Promising herself she'd make it up to Witch later, she returned her attention to Nick. "What you did or didn't get right isn't the point."

"Then what is the point?"

"The point is that we can't let the summer air and a starry night confuse us."

"Who's confused?"

Mercy wanted to scream with frustration. Nick was so good at derailing conversations, at making her doubt her common sense. Since the moment he stepped over her threshold, fire alarms had been going off in her bloodstream. If she didn't put out the fire pronto, she'd end up just like her parents—another burned-out casualty of raging hormones.

Gritting her teeth, she told him, "*Both* of us are confused. Everything about you is too much, too soon. You said yourself you didn't know what you wanted from me. When I opened that door last week, neither one of us expected the other. What you really need is a friend, Nick. Someplace to fit in again. I can be your friend, but I'm not ready to be anything else. I can't."

"You won't."

"All right, have it your way. I won't." She folded her arms across her chest.

"Why?"

"You're not my type," she lied smoothly.

Nick raised an eyebrow and mirrored her body language by folding his arms across his chest as he rocked the swing gently. "Ah, *chère*, you gonna have to learn to tell better lies."

Clenching her fists, Mercy ground out, "If you had the good sense to accept defeat gracefully, I wouldn't have to tell them at all!"

"Does that mean I am your type?"

"No, it does not. I don't have a type," she told him flatly, resigned to the fact that winning an argument with Nick was a lot like spinning around in a circle and then trying to walk a straight line.

"That's what Sister said." Nick nodded as if his suspicions had been sadly confirmed. "That you didn't know your type."

Mercy began a count of ten. When she reached nine, she blew out the breath she'd been holding and began to speak very slowly. "Nick, I'm not sure what Sister has been telling you, but never having been married does not make me a charter member of the Louisville Lonely Hearts Club. *And*"—she emphasized her point with a raised index finger—"while I'm sure this news is going to burst your macho bubble, I think you ought to know that technically I'm not entitled to wear white at weddings!"

"I have been wondering a bit about that point."

Mercy's mouth worked for a moment before she could force out anything. "Well, now you can stop wondering! I'm not some sad little spinster, so you can call off the little 'rescue mission' you and Sister Aggie have cooked up."

"Cooked up? You make that sound like Sister and I are conspirin' against you." Nick pushed the swing as though he were enjoying himself. "You don't really believe that, now, do you?"

"Only because you are," she informed him sweetly.

"Not us, darlin'. It's very hard to plot when the plotters don't agree."

Knowing she'd be sorry, but unable to contain her

curiosity, Mercy had to ask, "And what specifically don't you two agree about?"

"About you and Mr. Right. She thinks you've been looking for love in all the wrong places."

Mercy let that sink in for a moment while she ran her long nails through her hair like a comb, pulling the strands away from her face. "And what do you think?"

"I don't think you've been lookin' for Mr. Right at all." Nick stood up and smoothed his jeans down his thighs before he continued, "In fact, I don't even think you've been lookin' for Mr. Right Now."

Nick knew he'd hit the proverbial nail squarely on the head when her chin lifted sharply. Another little piece of the puzzle slipped into place. No doctors. No marrying men. No chemistry. Nothing that would challenge her nice, safe, little life. She never had answered his question about which scared her the most—the consummation of lust or the possibility of love. Until now, that is. He walked toward her, stopping in front of her, noting her lips had parted slightly and her breathing was shallow and a jot too rapid.

He knew he could kiss her if he wanted, that she expected him to, was probably afraid he would. As Nick looked down into blue eyes darkened with concern, he realized why lust scared her, and the answer surprised him. Gently, he said, "Mercy Malone's not looking for Mr. Right for the exact same reason she doesn't want to move to Pittsburgh."

To her credit, Mercy didn't flinch at his pronouncement. "Okay, Dr. Freud, let's hear it," she told him hoarsely. "Exactly why am I avoiding Prince Charming and committing career suicide?"

"You're gonna love this." Nick laughed and started down the steps, turning on the bottom one. "You're avoiding the Prince and Pittsburgh because you are scared to death you might upset the applecart."

"And what is that supposed to mean?"

"You worship the status quo. No gain, no pain."

Mercy's eyes narrowed, and he could tell her temper was beginning to heat up by the way she raised her voice when she said, "If you're going to spout clichés, then at least get them right! It's supposed to be—no pain, no gain."

"Naw, not for you, *chère*. No gain, no pain is exactly right. No risk, no hurt. Like I said before, you are one very pretty coward." He turned away and started for his car without waiting for a response. He'd stirred Mercy up. Now it was time to put the lid back on and let her simmer some more. Silence reigned for a second or two, and then he swore he heard the sound of her foot colliding with the wooden porch. Twice.

"If I'm such a coward, then why the hell do you keep coming back?" she hollered as he walked away.

When he pulled open his car door, he stared at her, taking in the tension in her posture, the way she leaned forward as if his answer mattered too much. Before he disappeared inside his car, he said, "I keep coming back because you make me forget."

Dropping his keys onto the nightstand, Nick fell back against the king-size bed. For once, the monotonous whirl of the ceiling fan's rosewood blades didn't irritate him. After an evening with Mercy, he needed the calm, rhythmic droning to help him unwind.

Nick dragged himself up long enough to shuck his clothing and then flipped out the lights. Not that he expected to get much sleep. Three weeks ago he hadn't been sleeping because of the silence in his life, and now he'd lie awake half the night because he couldn't get the image of long legs out of his mind.

Anticipation of future evenings with the real woman in his fantasies threatened to start the flow of adrenaline he usually felt only in the ER. After all this time he'd rejoined the living only to fall for the Queen of the Dead. *Dieu!* It felt good to want something again.

He wanted Mercy. He wanted so many slices of life he'd forgotten about. Like finding two toothbrushes in the bathroom and that someone had used the last clean towel. He wanted someone to ask him for a glass of water "while he was up." On cold mornings, he'd like to roll over and warm his nose in the tender flesh of Mercy's neck. He wanted to fight over who the dog loved more. Suddenly he was greedy for another human being after years of rationing his involvement with women, with people.

While the ceiling fan spun above him the wheels of his mind began to turn, and he looked for ways to solve the problem of getting Mercy to drop her defenses. Eventually, he'd get past her prejudice against doctors, but that wasn't the biggest stumbling block. Not by a long shot.

He didn't need a rocket scientist to tell him that two parents plus six marriages equaled the answer to Mercy's reluctance. Her folks had been married six times, and only *once* to each other. Thinking back on the conversation, he remembered she'd delivered that bit of information like the punch line of a joke. Her whole flip, sarcastic attitude about the subject of her parents' broken relationships was about as subtle as waving a bright red emotional flag. No, he didn't need a rocket scientist to draw him a diagram of Mercy's secrets.

Nick put his hands behind his head, pleased that he had a handle on the mystery of Mercy Malone. "I don't care how smoothly she tells the story, or how many jokes she makes, those failed marriages bother her more than she wants anybody to know."

Suddenly Nick frowned. *What* bothered her was only half the equation. The other half was *why?* What the hell did her parents' failures have to do with her? Being a poor judge of character wasn't listed as a genetic trait the last time he checked a medical textbook. Besides, Mercy didn't need to worry about making a mistake. At least, not this time. Not with him.

Nick closed his eyes and refused to listen to the nagging voice of reason inside his head. His good sense was in a snit over the fact that he'd up and decided to get serious about a woman he'd seen a grand total of three times. Well, in a roundabout way, I have spent the night with her already, Nick qualified, and yawned. And I'll be seeing her again tomorrow afternoon at the station.

Chaos greeted Nick as he approached the faux marble counter manned by the television station's receptionist. Before he could do more than get his name out, a harried young man rushed out of a door to Nick's left, the receptionist grabbed for a stack of papers that fluttered off the top of her computer workstation, and Mercy walked through a door on his right.

"Charlotte," warned the twenty-something black man. "Don't tell me it's not here! I saw the truck."

Charlotte triumphantly waved a fat overnight-express packet. "This?"

"Come to Papa," he said as he snatched the packet out of the girl's hands. The man let his breath out in a relieved whistle before he left with the package clutched in both hands, heaping curses on what Nick assumed was another television station.

"Problem?" Nick asked the woman behind the counter.

She grinned and answered, "Absolutely, positively not anymore."

"What she means is that Frank's been sweating bullets since Friday," Mercy said without making eye contact. "That's when Frank wanted to work on the Monday-night late show and realized we didn't have it yet."

"Then why did you schedule it?" Nick asked, and fought the urge to look down and see what was so darned interesting about his left shoulder that Mercy stared at it.

"We didn't," Charlotte told him. "The program exec did, and Frank's the worrying kind. Now that he's finally got the tape in his hands, he can edit all the local and national commercials on to one nice tape with the movie so that the late crew doesn't have to juggle three machines tonight."

Nick eyeballed the brass-trimmed wall clock behind the workstation. "Leaving it a little late, isn't he? It's four o'clock now. I hope he wasn't planning to leave at five o'clock like the rest of the world."

"He'll get it done." Charlotte's tone held supreme confidence. "We call him Mr. Impossible. Don't let the plastic pocket protector fool you. Frank's not as spastic as he appears."

"He has this phobia about biked tapes. Especially when someone drops the ball. It's happened to him before." Mercy motioned toward the way she'd entered. "Dan's already waiting for us in the conference room."

"Ladies first," Nick said as he reached to hold the edge of the dark green door. The small fantasy he'd been harboring about her eagerly awaiting his arrival evaporated completely. She slipped into the corridor without ever looking him directly in the eyes or acknowledging last night's kiss by so much as a blush. Since last night was out as a topic of conversation, he asked, "What exactly does 'biked' mean?"

"Biking. Like bicycling," she elaborated, using the bland tone of a museum guide. "That's what we call it when one station forwards a videotape to another station."

Nick digested her answer and her attitude. Mercy was every inch the detached professional, right down to the shoes that matched her blue silk suit, which was the exact color of the delicate, faded indigo blues of Cajun cloth. One of these days, he'd show her the few family heirlooms he had, like the rough, hand-made blanket of Cajun cloth that he kept in a trunk.

He wanted to whistle as he watched her glide down the corridor, hips gently swaying. Had they been anywhere else, he might have complimented Mercy's suit and told her about his *grandmère*'s passion for weaving, but for now, he decided to take his cue from her and stick to impersonal topics. Or try to. The station was her turf, and he could respect her need to keep her private life private. That didn't mean he had to like censoring his conversation.

With as much pretended interest as he could muster, he asked, "Mercy, now why would another station send you their movie?"

"They're not sending us *their* movie. Television stations don't own the movies we show. We have to pay whoever owns the rights if we want to run a movie. Well, sometimes we get them for free." When the corridor branched in two directions, Mercy tossed him a look over her shoulder to make sure he was following. Her gaze landed somewhere in the vicinity of his third shirt button.

Instead of grabbing her and tilting her chin up until she had to notice him, as he wanted to do, he reminded himself of their surroundings and stuck to shoptalk. "Why would someone give you a movie for free if you usually pay for them?"

"Because we agree to run the national advertising spots they've already sold and that are already on the tape. It's sort of a package deal." She turned right and climbed a flight of stairs.

He trailed her up the steps, wondering how long they could drag out this conversation before resorting to small talk about the weather. "I might not know much about television, but even I know it's damn hard to make money if you don't sell advertising."

She latched onto his interest like a man mired in quicksand grabbed hold of swamp vine. "The national ads only fill about half of the advertising slots. We make our money by selling the remaining ten or so minutes of commercial time."

"Ah." Nick nodded, suppressing a grin at Mercy's game effort to pretend that this was a perfectly natural conversation for two people who'd recently been necking on her front porch.

Mercy was trying so hard to ignore the chemistry between them that she only succeeded in increasing the tension swirling in the air currents. Being ignored was beginning to grate on his nerves. He controlled his irritation by reminding himself that this trip to the station was for the fund-raiser and had nothing to do with their relationship.

Noting the stiff carriage of her body, he swatted the conversational ball back into her court. "And what do you do with the movies when you're through with them?"

"That depends on how we get them. The program exec does all the buying, and he decides how we take delivery of the programming." She rattled on, not bothering to wait for a question this time, picking up speed as she went. "Sometimes we pull them off the satellite and then erase the tape. Sometimes we get a tape from whoever owns the film, which we then have to send back or bike it on to the next station that has the window to show that film."

When she paused a fraction of a second for breath, Nick knew he had to stop her before she stripped her vocal cords. Besides, she still hadn't *looked* at him, and she obviously wasn't going to unless he forced the issue. "Okay, that's it. Mercy—"

She cut him off as she paused in front of a door and announced, "Here we are."

"All right," he muttered in surrender. "Lead the way. I am perfectly willing to follow you to the ends of the earth, and it looks like that's what it's gonna take to get your attention," Nick told her earnestly, hoping the line would rattle her composure a bit. It did.

Mercy stopped right in the middle of knocking, and turned to truly look at him for the first time since he'd left her house the night before. Her baby blues widened, rounded, and blinked once before they settled into staring at him with apprehension.

"Looks like I won't have to go to the ends of the earth after all. I seem to have your attention. If your eyes were brown," Nick mused quietly, "you'd look like a deer caught in headlights."

She blinked again and found her voice. "You're mistaken, Nick. This is my impression of a silent-film heroine, strapped to the railroad track, and with no choice but to watch the shiny black, smoke-belching train barrel down on her as she struggles vainly against the inevitable."

"Then why worry? The hero always saves the heroine just in the nick of time."

"In the *nick* of time?"

"Bad pun?"

"Yeah. Really bad."

"Cut me some slack, *chère*. I haven't had to be clever in a long time. I'm out of practice."

"I thought we settled this last night." She knocked on the door and said, "You're wasting your time, Nick. You should practice on someone who cares."

"Oh, but I am!"

Mercy didn't have time to answer because a gruff voice from beyond the door ordered them to stop standing around the hallway shootin' the breeze. The door was jerked open and filled by a mountain of a man who topped Nick's six-foot three-inch height by several inches.

"You must be that Cajun doctor with the emergency."

"That'd be me," Nick allowed.

"You've got twenty minutes to sell me on this shindig of yours. But I'm telling you straight out, the station has already slotted more public-service programming and PSAs than last year. I'm going to take some convincing."

"Well, it's really Mercy's party," Nick said. "I'm just sort of coming along for the ride. She can explain how the station can help much better than I can."

For all his grizzly-bear posturing, Dan Harris, the station manager, was a pushover. Nick enjoyed watching Mercy play him like a two-bit piccolo. The meeting lasted far longer than twenty minutes and ended with a handshake and his promise to "get behind the project in every way possible."

"That was painless," Nick commented as soon as they were out of earshot of Dan.

"I told you it would be"—she allowed a little pride to creep into her voice—"if we did it my way."

"Let's hope the meeting with Kentucky Parents will be as easy," he cautioned, tossing out the baited hook.

"Why wouldn't it?"

"Because they're a volunteer group." *Wiggle the hook and see if she's interested.*

"And . . ."

She's interested. Keep it casual. Don't scare her off.

Nick rubbed the back of his neck as though he were perplexed by a huge problem. "I called them first thing this morning, but it looks like we're gonna have some trouble getting everyone on their board together. The president's a very busy family-law attorney."

"I'd guess custody would have to come before charity."

Wait and let her take the bait, Nick cautioned himself. "Yeah. Her schedule during the day is pretty tight for the next month."

"Well, mine's not." Even in such a short time, Mercy knew she had invested too much effort in the project to let little details bog it down. "If they're willing to help, the least I can do is make myself available whenever their board can meet."

Hook, line, and sinker! Time to reel her in.

"Good. I thought you'd feel that way." Nick checked the time on his wristwatch. "I didn't think the meeting with Harris would last this long. We've got to get moving if we're gonna make it across town in time."

At his cryptic words, suspicion clanged noisily in Mercy's head. She should have known that Nick was up to something. He'd let her off much too easily today considering how they'd parted last night, and now she knew why. All along he'd had Plan B waiting in the wings. Bracing herself, she asked, "In time for what?"

"Dinner. Our meeting with Susan Alastair, the busy attorney, and the Kentucky Parents board."

Mercy stopped before they reached the door to the reception room and crossed her arms. "You've scheduled a meeting without even checking with me?"

"Yeah. I'm a nineties kind of guy. I have opposable thumbs and an independent thought process. Let's go."

Pulling away from his extended hand, she told him, "Maybe I have plans."

"What happened to 'I'll make time'?"

"Maybe I made plans before I said that!"

Nick frowned and decided that jealousy was a forgotten emotion that he didn't particularly care to recollect. Her blue eyes held his, but their depths didn't offer the slightest hint as to whether she was bluffing or if she really had someplace to go. Someone to go to.

"Do you have plans?" he asked bluntly.

When she hesitated, Nick made a frustrated snort and rolled his eyes. "I'm not asking you to endure torture, just dinner. *Mon Dieu!* We won't even be alone. There'll be four other people, one of whom is a peace cop . . . a police officer. If I try anything funny, you can have me arrested. So do you have plans or not?"

"No. Not really," Mercy admitted. As soon as that smug, confident smile lit up Nick's face again, she wished she'd lied. Not that lying would have done much good. He always seemed to be able to tell.

"Good." He nodded in relief and approval. "We'll go in my car."

"No!" Going with Nick to dinner felt too much like accepting a real date. Separate cars would be a better idea. "You don't seriously expect me to ride in that loud, dangerous, adolescent contraption? You said no torture."

Nick pushed open the door to the reception area, which was empty now that quittin' time had come and gone. As Mercy passed him he said, "I wasn't aware it was torture to sink into leather seats and let your body soak up the vibration of power beneath you. It's an experience, I'll grant you. But not torture." Nick slapped his forehead. "Aw, I forgot you're not much on new experiences."

Having endured enough shots to her ego in the last week and a half, Mercy whirled in the middle of the lobby, ready to fight. "Is there anything about me you do like? I mean, you've taken potshots at my plumbing, my dining-room chairs, my house, my lack of garlic, and you call me a coward every time I see you! It's like you're trying to get a rise out of me!"

"Seems only fair. You sure as hell get a rise out of me!"

"Oh." Her lips formed the word, but she wasn't sure she'd actually said anything until Nick replied.

"Yeah. 'Oh' is right. Now stop fighting me every step of the way and just accept that I want to jump your bones. It sure will make conversation a helluva lot easier. We wouldn't have to argue about every little insinuation that way."

"We wouldn't have to argue at all if you'd forget about jumping my bones," she snapped.

"That ain't gonna happen, *chère*. And neither is anything else until you're ready."

Mercy tugged the blue silk jacket closed over her white camisole-style blouse and tried to figure out if Nick had the patience of a saint or if this was a clever ploy. Irritably, she said, "The only thing I'm ready for is to get this dinner over with. You drive if you want, but you'd better not so much as break the speed limit."

"Slow and easy, darlin'. On that you have my word."

A shiver rippled through her body at his promise, but she ignored it. Silently, she walked out to Nick's sleek, black Chevelle, but it wasn't until she'd settled back into the seat and Nick turned over the engine that she knew she'd made a major tactical error.

EIGHT

Nick's car assaulted her senses in a way that was purely sexual and impossible to ignore, much like the man himself.

She heard as well as felt the rumble of power created by the engine, the heart of Nick's sleek machine. An incredible leather seat welcomed her body as though the spot had been made for her. Nick's strong bronzed hands handled the stick shift and the steering wheel so sensually that Mercy was forced to lick her dry lips.

Before she made a fool of herself, she took her eyes off his hands and busied herself inventorying the contents of the front seat. A small wooden crate designed to hold cassette tapes balanced precariously on the console between them. Not surprisingly, Nick's taste ran to hot, electric jazz, and zydeco, which she knew was Cajun soul music. On the dashboard lay an opened pack of cinnamon gum, confirming her suspicion that Nick liked everything hot—from gumbo to gum.

His preference for "hot" explained why he'd been attracted to Midnight Mercy, but not why he spent so much time with Mercy May, fixing her plumbing and screen door, walking her dog, and cooking dinner. Sometimes when he didn't think she was looking, she saw that sadness he tried to hide. He said she made him forget. Forget what? The pain of losing his family? Being a stranger in a new city? The pressures of his career?

As they drove she admitted to herself that Nick's career was an unresolved emotional issue rattling around inside her. Her logical brain reminded her of rule number three—never trust a doctor with your heart—and her heart told her the time had come to ignore rule number three. Looking at his incredible profile, Mercy tried to drum up some of her ingrained prejudice against doctors as companions, but she couldn't.

Even if she disregarded the great biceps, smoldering black eyes, and killer Louisiana smile, she could not manage to make herself think of him as a doctor. Nick Devereaux wasn't like any doctor she'd ever met. In the last week and a half she'd spent more time with him than she had with her parents in four months.

If he was concerned about his reputation or image, he certainly didn't show it. Despite his comment about making less money in emergency medicine than in some of the high-dollar medical specialties, Mercy knew he could still have afforded a prestige car if he had wanted one. Obviously, he hadn't. Instead of a status symbol, he'd chosen to rebuild an old car that held fond memories of his youth.

He didn't carry a beeper and hardly talked about

medicine at all. He'd seemed detached that day in the emergency unit, yet she knew he cared deeply about the hospital and his patients. Why else would a doctor devote this kind of time to a hospital benefit? Why else would Sister Agatha approve of him? *Whoa!* Mercy cautioned herself. *The man is not a saint.* She'd better remember that this fund-raiser killed two birds with one stone for Nick. He was providing the hospital with a much-needed influx of cash and providing himself with a dandy reason to place himself squarely in her life now that she had committed to helping.

"You okay?" Nick asked, interrupting her reverie.

Startled, she looked up guiltily and said, "Fine."

"Fine? I don't think so. You're too quiet for fine, Mercy," he told her with a shake of his head. "Papa Jack said, 'Never trust a quiet woman. It's only the calm before the storm.'" Nick paused to negotiate a turn before telling her, "All that silence on your side of the car has got me scared about the storm you're busy brewin' over there."

Mercy made a noise that was part laugh and part huff. "You're not worried about any storm I might be brewing. I don't think you've ever been scared by anything."

"Now that's where you're wrong."

"Oh, really? Then what scares a big ol' hunk of man like you?" She angled a little bit to avoid straining her neck to see his expression. "Besides Sophie," she said.

He grinned and answered, "Snakes."

"Oh, come on. You don't expect me to believe that. Every boy I ever knew loved icky, slithery things like snakes."

"Well, I don't. I hate 'em. Always have. Always will."

Mercy was floored by the seriousness of his answer. He wasn't teasing about this. "But you grew up surrounded by a swamp and snakes!"

"So? You grew up with doctors, and you hate them."

"Touché." Mercy winced at having left herself open for his verbal right hook. "You got me. If I can dislike doctors, you can dislike snakes."

"Ah, *chère*, I don't just dislike snakes. I absolutely hate 'em. Surprised the hell out of my mother early one September when she realized I'd been spending all my free time in the swamp." He turned to watch her face as he said, "I mean *in* the swamp. Catching baby copperheads."

For a moment Mercy just stared at him slack-jawed. Then she snapped her mouth shut and asked, "What in heaven's name for? You said you hate snakes!"

Nick chuckled as he remembered his mother's reaction had been similar to Mercy's. "I was on a mission."

"Why?"

"Baby copperheads grow up to be adult copperheads, and I was a helluva lot more scared of the adults than I was the babies."

"You were crazy! Or stupid. Or both. Why would you want to catch them at all?" she asked, totally mystified by the convoluted logic of young boys. "They're poisonous!"

"That's exactly why I caught them. I thought I could eventually get rid of all the copperheads if I kept their young from growing up and reproducing."

Mercy sat in awed silence for a moment, before she commented. "Of course, total annihilation. Why didn't I think of that? Nothing else would do for Nick Devereaux. Didn't it occur to you that besides being dangerous, getting rid of the snakes in a swamp was like trying to fill up a swimming pool with a thimble?"

"I was ten, *chère*. All I knew was somebody had to do something. It seemed worth a shot. I've always liked a challenge."

Those last words were aimed at her, and Mercy felt her cheeks begin to flush with heat. "I believe you've mentioned that before."

"I thought I'd mention it again."

"No need," she assured him primly. "I am very much aware that you're an all-or-nothing kind of man. Black and white. No shades of gray. No holds barred." Mercy changed the subject before he could reply. "How much farther to the restaurant?"

"As a matter of fact, we're there. I mean here," he corrected.

Nick smoothly pulled into the parking lot and mentally chewed on her opinion of him as he killed the engine. She'd nailed his personality all right. Black or white. All or nothing. He couldn't have defended himself even if she'd given him the chance, because the woman was correct. He'd had years of nothing, and now he wanted it all.

A hostess led them through the dimly lit upscale Italian restaurant. Strings of tiny white lights, reminiscent of terrace al fresco dining, hung from the exposed rafters, and each table was covered with layers of starched white tablecloths that could be whisked away one by one as the tables were reset for new guests. Their party was the only group in a room filled with couples.

The hostess left them with the promise to send a waiter right over. Introductions were made in a round-robin fashion as Nick pulled out a chair for Mercy and apologized to the four people, "Sorry; our meeting ran longer than expected."

"We really are sorry." Light from table candles flickered as Mercy added warmly, "I hope all of you haven't waited to order because of us?" She groaned as four heads bobbed in response to her question. "I feel terrible now! Will you forgive us if I tell you the meeting was worth every extra minute it ran over."

A brunette whose voice sounded like a foghorn asked, "Does that mean good news?"

"The best. We're in business. The station has agreed to give us the airtime and sponsor either a disk jockey or live music for the dancing."

Murmurs of approval echoed from around the table as Nick took his own seat, between Mercy and Susan Alastair, the statuesque president of Kentucky Parents for Better Health. When he glanced around the table, he wanted to kick himself for being in such a rush to get Mercy settled. If he hadn't been in such a hurry, he wouldn't have pulled out the first available chair. He wouldn't have plopped Mercy down right next to a man who was obviously either a single guy looking to get lucky or a married guy without a ring but with roamin' in his eyes. Either way, Nick wasn't happy about the situation.

Susan leaned forward, adjusted her stylish wire-rim glasses, and said, "Miss Malone, I'm sure I speak for all the board when I tell you that we appreciate your allowing us to participate in Ghouls' Nite Out."

"Please, call me Mercy. And don't thank me, thank Nick. This fund-raiser is his baby."

"It might be my baby, but it's going to be a short pregnancy," Nick announced firmly. "Mercy wants us to pull off this shindig by mid-August."

"Wow. That's quick," uttered the man on Mercy's left, and casually looped an arm around her chair. "But I want you to know that I'm willing to do whatever it takes."

His little speech sounded like the screech of a car alarm to Nick. Very deliberately, he caught the guy's beady little snake eyes and stared him down, silently warning him that if he didn't move that arm, he'd be wearing a cast on it. Under Nick's watchful eye, the man—Paul, he thought—gingerly removed his arm and fiddled with his menu.

When the waiter appeared, Nick relaxed his vigil and stared at his own menu. Uncomfortably, he wondered if Mercy had noticed his slight slip into Neanderthal territory. She wouldn't thank him for his macho display. No, Mercy wasn't ready to admit he had the right to wine and dine her much less lay claim to her like some caveman.

In the absence of any pointed looks shot in his direction, Nick assumed he was safe for now and breathed a small sigh of relief as he gave the waiter his order. After that, conversation and dinner were both served up at the speed of light. Nick enjoyed himself now that he was sure Paul, the overly friendly peace cop, had gotten the message about whom Mercy would be leaving with tonight. In fact, all he had to do was simply lean back in his chair and watch Mercy go to work.

She genuinely liked people, which made it easier for her to charm them into doing whatever she needed. And when people already wanted to help, it was like shooting fish in a barrel for someone with Mercy's finesse. By the time dinner wound up, most of the details had been decided and delegated. The white tablecloth was speckled with red sauce, red wine, and assorted seafood-pasta sauces.

All of the board except Susan begged off dessert to head home to their children and spouses. When the commotion of departures had cleared, Susan and Mercy agreed to split one of the restaurant's awe-inspiring concoctions of Kahlúa, pecans, and praline ice cream. When the dessert arrived, the three of them were chatting as comfortably as old friends. The women nibbled at the enormous dessert and ironed out a few inconsequential details while Nick glanced around the room, trying to figure out why he had that creepy feeling of being stared at.

He almost laughed as he realized that he was being enviously stared at by the men in the room because he happened to be enjoying dessert with two beautiful women. Little did they know that Nick would have been more than happy to share his good fortune as long as they didn't expect him to share the dark-haired temptress on his left. While he might admire Susan's style, she didn't do a thing for his pulse rate.

On the other hand, looking at Mercy made him

want to jump right out of his skin and into hers. Although she'd rather die than admit it, he suspected it was the same for her. She'd tried so hard to look completely different from Midnight Mercy today, but that thin white blouse she wore beneath her suit had been giving him fits for the last few hours. He wanted to know how the silklike fabric would feel beneath his hands as he caught a handful and tugged it out of her waistband.

Susan's cultured voice snatched his attention away from the fantasy. "I like this idea about getting corporations to sponsor the table decorations. Fresh flower centerpieces are horribly expensive; the less we spend the more we make for the hospital. I can get my assistant to give us a list of likely companies."

"We're going to have upward of two hundred tables, Susan," Mercy said. "That's a lot of companies."

"Not so many. You'd be surprised how many business contacts you make handling family law. Family-owned corporations and partnerships are the major bones of contention in a lot of my divorce cases."

"I would have thought the children would be," Mercy said in surprise.

"Unfortunately, the children are only bargaining chips to some parents. You know, one spouse will say to the other, 'You can't have the children unless . . .'"

"That's a rotten way to treat a child," Nick said.

"Yeah, it is," Susan agreed. "But divorce is such a bitter time in most people's lives that they can't think past tomorrow's revenge."

"How sad that must be for them," Mercy whispered. "Wait a minute! What am I talking about?

How horrible for you. I can't imagine having to work with adults who spend all their time creating misery." She leaned closer to Nick to reach the dish as she carefully fished for a spoon of ice cream and nuts. "I never gave it much thought before, but I'd guess being a divorce lawyer is a pretty stressful way to earn a buck. I doubt you get much call to referee 'amicable' divorces."

"Ha!" Susan waggled her spoon in the air. "There is no such thing as an 'amicable' divorce. Civilized maybe, but not amicable, at least not during the divorce process. Amicable comes later, sort of like perspective, but during the divorce, it hurts like hell. For at least one of them. The one who believed in forever."

The one who believed in forever. How could you not believe in forever, if you believed in love? A little shiver slipped up Mercy's spine and raised the hairs on the back of her neck. "Whatever happened to 'until death us do part'?"

"MTV," Susan quipped. "No one in America has an attention span of more than ten seconds." Turning toward Nick, she asked, "What about you? You haven't said much. Stop practicing your impression of the strong, silent type and tell me if you agree with my rock-video diagnosis as the cause of divorce."

"I wouldn't dare disagree." He grinned at her. "Seems to me that you're the expert."

"Now, I thought a doctor, of all people, would know what causes broken hearts." Susan looked back and forth between the two of them. "What? What'd I say that was so funny?"

"Private joke. You had to be there," Mercy told

her, amazed that she could remember that first uncomfortable conversation with Nick and think it was funny. She looked at him and their eyes locked. Suddenly an amusing memory turned into the realization that they now had shared history. One of the most compelling bonds was the bond created by memories, the ability to turn to someone and say, "Remember when . . . ?"

She had to accept the fact that every moment she spent with him was going to create more memories. Some intimate, some funny, some intense, and she was very much afraid some would be sad, unless she was very, very careful with her heart.

"Well, are you going to keep me in suspense or what?" Susan demanded.

"It loses a little something in the telling," Nick explained, his gaze still on Mercy. Knowing he had to break the spell of intimacy that threatened to engulf him, he dragged his attention away from the questions and promises he saw reflected in the blue depths of Mercy's eyes. To the other woman he said, "Have you ever been divorced, counselor?"

"Are you kidding? In order to be divorced, first I would have to find a man who could put up with me long enough to propose and marry me."

"You couldn't be that hard to take," Mercy chided. She couldn't imagine how a bright, beautiful, articulate woman like Susan could have any trouble finding the right man.

"Trust me. I'm never home, and I want everything yesterday. I'm rarely tactful. I bribe my secretary and paralegal with fat bonuses so they won't leave me for a kinder boss. Who'd want me?"

"Try again, Susan," Nick told her. "You're talking to someone who knows you've got a soft spot in your heart for people in need. You're the president of and driving force behind Kentucky Parents."

"Well, it's not like I invented the organization! I got involved with the group because one of my clients was feeling a little guilty about not doing his share for the less fortunate of this world. He had money but no time, and asked me to find a charity he could throw all that guilty money at. I found Kentucky Parents and liked it so much I stayed around."

"At least he threw money. Most people leave it at 'I'd like to help, but I just can't find the time,' " Nick remarked. "Every day it's a race to see who can use up all the hours in the day first. People pack so much into their schedules they don't have any time left over to remember things like anniversaries, birthdays, or even if they fed the cat."

"Like my parents," Mercy agreed.

Susan pushed the bowl of ice cream toward Mercy and shook her head to indicate she didn't want any more. "That sounds perfectly ominous and like a story begging to be told. What's wrong with your parents?"

"Take my name, for instance. It's a perfect example."

"Okay," Nick agreed slowly. He drew his brows together. "You were named for Mercy Hospital. What does that have to do with anything?"

Mercy swirled the melting ice cream with her spoon. "I was named Mercy not because of my parents' attachment to the hospital, but because it was easy to remember. I got my middle name, May, for the same reason. Mercy May Malone. Guess which month I was born in?"

"They didn't!" exclaimed Susan, trying her best not to laugh.

"They did. Mercy May Malone. Mom never missed a birth month. She never got the birth*day* right, but she always remembered it was sometime in May. All she had to do was get mad at me and say, 'Mercy May!' in that disapproving parental tone, and you could see it in her eyes. That horrified I've-got-to-get-my-daughter-a-birthday-present look. So don't laugh, Susan! If you think it's so funny, tell us your middle name. Everyone hates their middle names."

"I don't. Honest. Susan Elizabeth Alastair. All perfectly normal and plain." She looked directly at Nick and gave him a tiny half smile that was almost flirty. Mercy didn't have any trouble reading the invitation in the other woman's eyes. In a voice that was much too low for Mercy's taste, Susan prompted, "Your turn, Nick."

He didn't answer right away. Instead he twisted his head to study Mercy, giving her the once-over, as if trying to decide if she could be trusted with his secret. Finally, he said, "Octave. Nicholas Octave Fontenot until Papa Jack Devereaux married my mother and adopted me."

"Octave?" Mercy's question was strained from the effort to accept the news calmly.

"Octave." He scooted his chair back a few inches and silently dared either woman to say a word.

"How colorful," Susan managed, and then she and Mercy lost the battle to suppress their laughter.

Nick might have taken offense except that Mercy

had placed her hand on his thigh, holding tight as she giggled through an apology. "It's a lovely name. Really. I'm sorry we're laughing."

"It's all right, *chère*." Graciously, Nick accepted her apology. "I just don't ever wanna hear it slip out in conversation."

At the moment he probably would have forgiven her for a multitude of sins. Whether Mercy realized it or not, she had finally taken a giant step in their relationship. Her hand rested naturally on his thigh. She'd reached out for him, touched him as though she had a right to, as though something more than friendship bound them together.

Any guilt Nick felt over warning off the cop evaporated. Both he and Mercy had staked a claim tonight. She'd just been more subtle about it. Nick watched Susan's eyes flick briefly over the sight of Mercy's hand on his thigh. Message received. It was a message he had no intention of contradicting.

Three more weeks. Three more weeks, Mercy chanted to herself as she sat down in Sister Agatha's office to wait for the nun. Three more weeks, and this benefit would be behind her. The end to her torture couldn't come a moment too soon. She desperately needed time away from Nick to regain her perspective, and that wasn't going to happen as long as they were working together on the benefit. Nick was a virus in her bloodstream that she couldn't seem to shake.

Grimacing, Mercy remembered that she had actually picked up the phone yesterday to check in with Nick. Not because she had to talk about the fund-raiser, but because somewhere along the line, Nick had become a good friend.

He showed up at the city of Haunt's Fourth of July picnic auction and bid fifty-two dollars for her picnic basket. To be completely honest, her heart tripped over itself when she heard his voice start the bidding. She had casually mentioned the picnic, but she hadn't expected him to be there. Not really. After all, her parents had never managed to make the school Christmas pageants or piano recitals; she was used to being the only one without family in the audience. She hadn't expected him to be any different than her parents, until he had been.

To make matters worse, her body's ridiculous physical lust for the man was getting all screwed up with her acceptance of him as a platonic part of her life. Lately, she felt like two people: One was scared to death of letting herself take that last step toward physical intimacy, and the other didn't care about anything but that delicious feeling that settled in the pit of her stomach when Nick was around.

Even when he wasn't around, she couldn't escape the thought of making love with Nick. If she had to watch that damn promo one more time, she thought she'd scream. Every time she turned the television on, there he was again! It wasn't that she minded sharing the spotlight. If only she hadn't had to share it with Nick.

Somehow, Caroline in publicity had gotten a look at Nick and made one of her famous snap decisions to use him in the promos. When she heard him speak, Caroline picked up the phone and talked a local advertising firm into donating their expertise for a series of television spots for Ghouls' Nite Out. Every blasted one of them featured voice-overs of Nick using that shamelessly sensual accent of his to sell tickets.

Hogwash! They're selling Nick, Mercy thought irritably.

In the first spot, all anyone could see was the sexy, dark outline of a well-built man waiting in the shadows at the edge of a swamp-surrounded graveyard, waiting to claim Mercy Malone on Ghouls' Nite Out. Waiting for his chance to come out of the eerie shadows created by moss-laden cypress trees and low-rising mist.

Each promo brought what the whole city was calling "the sexy swamp thing" closer to the full light of the moon, closer to a spellbound Mercy Malone, who leaned forlornly against an old graveyard monument. The camera closed in as she promised in an uncertain whisper that she was a match for anything, man or beast, that roamed the night. Every promo spot hinted at a tortured past, hidden evil, and one chance to reunite the lovers on Ghouls' Nite Out.

Every time she saw the damned thing she could feel the swirl of sexually charged mist as it wove around her legs; she could even hear Nick's promo slogan in her sleep. As the camera pulled back for a wide shot of the graveyard, Nick's earthy accent promised, "Sometimes, all a body needs is a little magic. Help us create some magic on Ghouls' Nite Out." In the promo the screen would fade to black, showing only the information on the event and a telephone number for ordering tickets. In her dreams, something else entirely happened.

"Argh!" Mercy growled, refusing to waste her time brooding about the fantasies that cluttered her sleep.

She couldn't even complain about the melodramatic commercials being a bad idea. Tickets were flying out of the offices of Kentucky Parents. At the rate they were being bought, the event would be a sellout by the end of the week. Before the station even started running the promo featuring a lusty kiss between the swamp thing and Mercy Malone.

Running the tip of a fingernail absently along her bottom lip, Mercy remembered doing that spot over and over, take after take, kiss after kiss. Flesh to flesh. As usual, she hadn't been wearing much of anything, and Nick wore only a pair of jeans that Caroline insisted were not indecently tight. Well, she wasn't belly to belly with the man. There wasn't a soul at the taping who didn't know exactly how Nick felt about kissing Mercy Malone. All they had to do was look below the waist. His jeans hid nothing.

When the door opened behind her, Mercy forced herself to put aside her troubling thoughts. She turned with a smile that froze on her face as Nick said, "Howdy, *chère.*"

At least he looked like a doctor today, in pale blue scrubs with a laminated hospital ID clipped to his pocket.

"Nick." She wasn't certain if his name came out as a greeting or a groan.

She hoped it sounded like a greeting, and she hoped he wouldn't notice the fact that her palms had started sweating the moment she saw him. Guilt most likely. Standing up, Mercy surreptitiously wiped her palms against the back of the white jeans she wore.

"Why are you here? Sister asked me to drop by after my show was taped and go over the complimentary invitations for the people who've made substantial cash donations."

"She's hung up in a meeting." Nick noticed the way she rubbed her hands against her rump and realized that Mercy was beginning to simmer quite nicely. Maybe the time had come to stir her up again. He hadn't kissed her since they shot the promos, weeks ago. *Dieu*, he'd wanted to, but he'd kept his hands and his lips to himself.

As he walked around the desk he said, "Sister asked me to look in her desk for the patrons' list. That is, if you don't mind going over the list with me?"

"No. No, of course not." *Liar*.

For the next half hour she made a pretense of paying attention to the list and nodding her head as Nick suggested the number of tickets for each patron. In the end, she picked up the list and said, "I don't see any problems. I'll get this right over to Kentucky Parents."

"No need to go rushin' round. Why don't we fax it?" Nick suggested as he pulled on the piece of paper that she clutched in a death grip.

"Oh. What a good idea. Why didn't I think of that?"

"Maybe because you were too busy trying to escape from me. You've perfected escape to an art form in the last week. I thought we were friends."

"I've been a little busier than usual is all."

"Right," Nick said, dragging out the word so that it sounded like an accusation as he flipped through the Rolodex and placed the list in the fax machine on the credenza. After he dialed, he waited for the tone and pushed the send button. "There. It's all done. All we have to do now is call and tell them what we just faxed over."

Picking up the regular phone receiver on the desk, he dialed the committee's office. "Janey? Hey, your fax machine should be spitting out a list of people who should be put on the free-invitation list. Yeah, that's right. These are the heavy hitters who made contributions straight to the fund set up at the hospital." He paused while Janey went to check her fax machine. "Yeah. That's it. The number of invitations they should get is in parentheses behind their name. Right. So how is everything going over there?"

Mercy saw her opportunity to slip out the door, and she attempted to take it. With a halfhearted wave good-bye, she picked up her small purse and slung it over her shoulder. Nick frowned at her and started to put his hand over the mouthpiece to tell her to stay, but before he could, he jerked his hand away and shouted "What!" into the phone.

Startled, Mercy froze. She hated bad news.

NINE

"Both hands?" Nick's eyes closed, and he shook his head gently. "When did you find out? Well, why didn't somebody call me yesterday?"

Nick made a gesture as though asking God to save him from fools. "He suggested a band? Have you checked them out? No? Where are they playing?" He grabbed a pad to write on. "Yeah, I know the place. Mercy Malone's here with me. If I can work it out, we'll catch a few sets tonight and make a decision on whether or not to go with live music. Let Susan and Paul know the plan."

Putting the phone down, Nick cursed fluently in Frengish, a Cajun combination of French and English, before he told Mercy what she'd already guessed from the phone conversation. "The disk jockey managed to break both his hands."

"How?"

"The *first* one while catching a baseball."

Mercy whistled. "Must have been some fastball."

"The *second* one when his wife slammed the van door on his good hand at the emergency room. *Dieu!* It's a little late to be scrounging around for entertainment, but I'd rather have a band than another deejay. So we gotta check out a band tonight."

"No, *we* don't have to check out a band. I didn't volunteer for the entertainment committee. Besides, you can't go anywhere. You're on duty until midnight or something."

Nick waved that objection aside. "I'll get Greene to cover for me. He owes me a few favors."

"Good, then you can go out clubbing. Me, I've got to get home to Witch. She's pregnant, and there is a limit to how much I can ask of her kidneys."

"Surely one of your neighbors knows where you keep the spare house key for emergencies like this one? No? Then I'll bet Sophie has a key of her very own. No way you gonna leave a pregnant dog without a backup baby-sitter. Am I right?"

Pursing her lips, Mercy grudgingly admitted, "Unfortunately."

Nick picked up the receiver. "Call her." When she hesitated, he prodded, "Come on, *chère*. Be a pal. Don't make me go alone. I guar-ran-tee you'll have a good time. If you want, I'll even teach you the Cajun two-step."

Walking over to the desk to snatch the receiver from his hand, Mercy punched in the number with a series of short jabs that punctuated her words. "Like I care whether or not you teach me anything! I'm only going because I've seen your cassette collection. Heaven knows what kind of band you'd hire if I didn't go along. Hello, Sophie . . ."

Mercy pulled into the gravel parking lot right behind Nick's Chevelle, cursing as her old Jaguar hit yet another pothole. When she got out of her car, she stared at the enormous weathered gray building that dominated the south side of the highway. A covered porch ran the length of the nightclub; barn-red double doors and shutters provided the only color on the drab-looking structure except for the big red neon letters across the roof. Unfortunately, a couple of letters were out, so the sign read AD BO 'S instead of BAD BOB'S.

What kind of band did Nick expect to find in a roadside honky-tonk that probably paid the band twenty-five dollars a night plus drinks? Her instincts had warned her the minute he told her the band was playing in a nightclub halfway between Haunt and Louisville.

As Nick walked up beside her she stated the obvious, "This is a roadhouse."

"Yeah, I know." Nick noted the tapping of her fingernails. "You got somethin' against sawdust and beer?"

"I'll let you know."

A couple came out the red doors, and Mercy studied the woman's clothes. Short, short, blue-jean cutoffs, cowboy boots, and a halter top. "At least you were right about there not being a dress code."

"Stop fishing for compliments," he told her as he took her by the elbow. "You look great."

Mercy rolled her eyes. She'd dressed to go straight home after her meeting at the hospital, not for going out—white jeans, a white men's cotton T-shirt, and white sneakers. "As compared to what? The Good-Humor man?"

"As compared to anything I've seen all day."

"Oh, right! You've been looking at nurses all day."

Nick hauled her around to face him. "I don't look at nurses. At least not the way I look at you."

To prove his point, he took his time perusing her from head to toe. His eyes burned into her each time they paused in their journey, making her want to pull away, but the anticipation fluttering in her stomach kept her rooted in place.

Nick noticed the way her jeans hugged her calves, the way the stark white T-shirt enhanced her slight tan even in the artificial light, and the way the belt called attention to her waist. *The belt.* Now, there was that one item of her attire that bothered him. "The belt I could live without."

Looking down at her slender, turquoise-studded belt, Mercy asked, "What's wrong with my belt?"

"It's the way you've got the excess looped back over the belt and hanging down. The tip of it's pointy and silver. It reminds me of a snake."

"Good," Mercy told him firmly, more in command of that flutter in her belly now that he'd criticized her. "Then maybe you'll be afraid to touch."

Laughing heartily, Nick said, "Not on your life, darlin'!" and pulled open the red doors. "After you. You do dance don't you?"

"With you? Only the fast ones."

"Now, why is that?" Tonight was going to be fun, Nick could tell already. "You afraid to get belly to belly again?"

Mercy ignored him and soaked in the panorama before her. An explosion of color flooded her line of vision as the couples on the dance floor swayed and whirled and separated. Beneath the thin soles of her sneakers, she could feel not only the uneven texture of the sawdust, but also the rocking rhythms of the band's music. The hardwood floors seemed to vibrate with life and energy.

Somewhere in the crowd she caught the sound of a beer bottle breaking. Immediately, everyone within hearing distance shouted "Ho!" like a two-syllable word and offered up a round of applause for the unfortunate waiter. Bartending noises—the whir of a blender, the rattle of glass and ice, and the sound of the cash register being slammed shut—echoed on her right, drawing her attention. Three men behind a ridiculously long slab of polished wood juggled liquor bottles and caused mixed drinks to appear magically almost before the patrons could finish ordering them.

The smells of beer, honest sweat, and smoke filled the air. Everything about the place teased her senses. She was amused by the contradiction in the club's dreary exterior and lively interior.

"How 'bout a drink?" Nick asked as he started for the bar.

"Bloody Mary, lots of salt, no stalk."

"Salt's bad for you."

"So are you, but I haven't given you up yet either."

"Good point," he agreed as he turned away. "Bloody Mary, lots of salt, coming right up."

Looking at his back, she made a bet with herself that Nick was most likely a Jack and Coke man. When he returned, she asked. He was, and she followed him to a table.

Scooting into a chair in the corner was a mistake because she had no maneuvering room. The good doctor saw her predicament as an opportunity to crowd right in next to her. For once she didn't mind, perhaps because they were on neutral ground.

While she nursed her drink, Nick cast his gaze around the room and his fingers through his hair. Mercy lowered her eyes, afraid she'd betray her thoughts, which were on the quick shower he took before leaving the hospital and how good he smelled when he came out. Sexy even, with his thick hair still slightly damp. He'd changed into chinos and a deep purple polo shirt, open at the neck.

Raising her eyes again, she was drawn to the gold chain and small medallion he always wore. It tantalized her as a ray of light caught it, making the lustrous metal wink at her, daring her to touch.

Giving in to the urge that she'd had since the morning he sat on the edge of her bed, Mercy reached out and lifted the medal. The underside was smooth against her fingertips and it was as warm as the skin she touched with the backs of her knuckles. She could feel Nick's watchful gaze on her as she asked, "Do you ever take this off?"

"No. It was a gift."

"It must mean a lot to you. I mean, if you wear it all the time."

"Yeah, it does."

She leaned closer to study the design on the gold circle. A man carried a walking staff in one hand and a small child on his shoulder. "St. Christopher, right?"

Nodding, Nick said, "Patron saint of children and travelers."

For a second Mercy saw the sad, lost look in Nick's eyes again. The fleeting shadow of melancholy came and went so quickly, Mercy might have believed she imagined it, except she hadn't. She'd seen that look too many times before. Suddenly she felt like she'd invaded his privacy, and she let the medallion drop. Although she wanted to ask more, she knew that now was not the time.

"What do you think of the band?" Nick asked abruptly, wanting to change the subject. He wasn't ready to tell her about the medal. Not yet.

"If you promise not to say I told you so, then I'll admit there is something about these guys that makes my feet tap and gets the adrenaline started. Even this set of slow ballads has me swaying with the music."

"I know. I found this place the night the *chaoui* came visitin'." Nick swirled the dark liquid in his glass. "I felt like driving, so I stayed off the interstate and took the scenic tour back to Louisville. And there it was in the middle of this old highway. From the outside it reminded me of a *fais-dodo*."

"What's that?"

Nick raised a brow and considered how to explain. "*Fais-dodo* is Cajun baby talk. It means 'go to sleep.'"

"I don't understand."

"That's how it translates, but what it *is* is a music hall. A place for the whole family to get together—aunts, uncles, brothers, sisters, cousins, parents, everyone." Nick gave her a crooked smile as he traced the edge of his glass with a fingertip. "Cajuns love extended family and any excuse to celebrate, even if we have to build a place to hold the whole family at one time."

"Like a personal nightclub?"

"Sure enough. Complete with band. A couple of instruments, even if it's nothing but an accordion and an old fiddle, constitutes a band in Lou'siana's French Triangle. And you'll always find a couple of impromptu spoon players to throw into the mix. Any Cajun family can muster a respectable band."

Grinning, Mercy said, "Must not be too respectable a band if the name of your music halls means go to sleep."

"Aw, now, *fais-dodo* has nothing to do with the music! Anytime you get family together, *chère*, you gonna have kids. The old halls were places for the kids to go to sleep and the grown-ups to play. When you build a party house"—Nick drew a rectangle on the table with his finger and divided it into two long rooms—"you make sure there's a room in the back to put all the kids to bed. The big, long room in front is for the music and the dancing."

He sectioned off a small part of the children's room. "Sometimes they make a second room in back for cards."

"Is that where you learned to play the cutthroat card game?"

"*Bourré.* By the time I was old enough to join the card games, we'd been in N'Awlins a long time. Besides, the old-style *fais-dodo* as a family entertainment was already fading when I was a boy. By the time I was eighteen, only a few of the bigger halls were left, like the one over in Breaux Bridge, which catered to the tourist trade mostly. So I didn't bother. It didn't have quite the same feeling as the family places I remembered."

"But what about your own extended family? Didn't you go back to the bayou for visits . . . or celebrations, or whatever?"

"Didn't have any family left to visit. Not blood family anyway." Nick polished off his drink. "Just Papa Jack, *Maman*, and Catherine."

"Catherine. That was your sister's name?"

"Yeah. It was."

Nick stood up and pulled her up so abruptly that Mercy grabbed his arm for balance. He lifted her chin and brushed his lips with hers. The sadness was back in his eyes again, and loneliness too.

"Dance with me, *chère*."

Without words, Mercy agreed. How could she not? Maybe this would mean as much to him as hearing his voice in the crowd at the picnic auction and knowing that he'd come to lend moral support. As he drew her into his arms on the dance floor, Mercy knew somehow that Nick had never missed a single one of Catherine's school plays, or piano recitals, or birthdays. Not this man.

Resting his cheek against her hair, he realized that for the first time he'd admitted out loud that he didn't have any family left. Not real family. Not like the family he'd lost. Right now he needed her so much, it scared him. The old black hole inside him threatened to swallow his soul again, and the only way he could fight it was by holding on to Mercy.

For once, she didn't fight him. She melted into his arms without a word, seeming to understand that—right now—the one thing he needed was her. Not witty conversation, not an argument, just her in his arms and next to his heart.

As they slowly glided around the floor, Nick knew he had fallen in love with Mercy, with her ramshackle house, and with her nosy neighbors. He'd gone looking for a woman to warm his bed and had stumbled over the woman who warmed his heart. *Dieu*, he'd fallen in love with a woman whose biggest emotional commitment to date had been the purchase of a house.

Regardless, he loved her. Whether or not Mercy loved him was another question entirely. He devoutly hoped that the answer would be yes, and considering the gentleness of the hand that rubbed his back, offering comfort, and the way she nuzzled her cheek against his chest, he had reason to hope.

"*Chère*, look up."

He felt rather than heard the slight intake of her breath, but she didn't pull away. Instead, she raised her face to his. Nick kissed her then, in the middle of the darkened dance floor. A quick, openmouthed kiss that did more taking than giving.

Dazed, Mercy couldn't open her eyes when Nick finally lifted his mouth from hers. Nick tasted of whiskey and passion, a heady combination. Seconds later she found Nick staring at her, waiting for her to make a decision. All of the longing of the past weeks had invaded her bones, making them rubbery and weak. All she could think about was Nick's confession of insomnia. Suddenly she didn't want him to go home alone, not tonight, but neither did she want him to mistake the change in their relationship for the promise of a future.

Shakily, she asked, "What about the band? Didn't we come here to talk to them?"

"I'll give them my card, and they can call me if they're interested. Let's go."

Her indecision must have shown on her face, because Nick whispered, "I won't take anything more than you're willing to give, *chère*. It's just you, and me, and tonight."

"What about tomorrow?" she asked quietly.

"Tomorrow's gonna take care of itself. Don't you worry. It always does. It always will."

The twenty-minute drive back to Haunt was the longest drive of Mercy's life. Alone in her car, she had plenty of time to convince herself that she was making a mistake, but she wasn't inclined to listen. In her heart she knew the point of no return had come and gone on that roadhouse dance floor. A woman's libido was only designed to take so much teasing before nature took control of the decision making. As she reached her driveway her nerves were ready to snap from the anticipation of what would come next.

Mercy managed to get out of her car calmly enough and up the steps of the porch, but she struggled to get the key into the lock. Nick hovered behind her, making it impossible for her to concentrate long enough to stop her hand from shaking. Wordlessly, he took the key from her and unlocked the front door. Once inside, Mercy let the strap of her purse fall off her shoulder and tossed the small bag onto the entryway table.

When the dog didn't meet them at the door, Nick asked, "Shouldn't Witch be here barking or something?"

Too nervous to look at Nick, Mercy inhaled and exhaled slowly before she told him, "No. Sophie said she'd take Witch back to her house tonight in case I got tied up."

Nick laughed, low and sensuous as he took her hand and led her up the stairs. "Now, that I can arrange. In fact, it'd be my pleasure. You did keep the stockings, didn't you?"

All the precious air in her lungs left in a hurry, leaving Mercy feeling slightly dizzy as they reached the second-floor landing. She felt like too much was happening, too slowly. Nick was acting like they had all the time in the world to indulge fantasies, but she'd been counting on him to make love to her quickly, out of a fierce need to end the suspense and tension between them.

That's what his kiss on the dance floor had promised, and now . . . now everything was different. Too much time to think, and not enough time to want. Mercy stared at her feet because she was afraid that if she looked at the overpowering man in front of her, she might embarrass herself by begging him to put her out of her misery.

"Nick—" she began.

"Hey." With a thumb and forefinger, Nick brought her chin up. He gave her a confident grin as he asked, "You don't have to worry. What kind of doctor would

I be if I wasn't prepared for emergencies? I've got it covered, so to speak."

When concern still clouded her eyes, Nick realized that protection wasn't all she was worried about. "Mercy May Malone, you're taking this whole deal much too seriously. This is Nick, darlin'. I know you're not Midnight Mercy, and I don't give a damn. I want you. I have wanted you since your sexy mouth fell open the first time I saw you. I thought I'd died and gone to heaven right there on your porch."

Mercy opened her mouth to protest, but Nick silenced her by laying two fingers across her lips. Despite his reassuring smile, she noticed the deep need in his eyes, like the hot coals of a carefully banked fire. He whispered, "Don't say anything. I'm trying to take this slowly. And I gotta tell you, it ain't easy."

When Mercy's tongue brushed deliberately against his fingertips, Nick cursed and replaced the fingers with his mouth. He had no other choice, not if she didn't want to take things slowly. They wanted each other, and within that passion there was no room for doubts or tomorrow or gentleness. He curled one hand around the nape of her neck and walked backward, still kissing her, into the bedroom. His other hand was already unfastening her studded belt, sliding it out of the loops with one smooth pull.

Its silver tip and buckle hit the hardwood floor a second later, and with it fell Mercy's inhibitions. Her hands returned the favor by removing his belt, and Nick broke the kiss only long enough to pull off her soft cotton T-shirt. Both hands cradled her head as he nipped her bottom lip and then sealed his mouth to hers, thrusting deeply when she opened for him.

His hands slid down her throat and over her shoulders, catching her bra straps and slipping them down. His mouth followed the trail of his hands, leaving a moist path along one collarbone as he worked loose the bra clasp in the back. Impatiently, he stripped the sheer undergarment away, freeing her breasts to his gaze and touch.

Mercy's breath came in ragged fits and starts as his wet mouth sucked one nipple. When he started to tip her onto the bed, Mercy refused. Right now, she wanted as much of him as he had of her. Grabbing fistfuls of his shirt at the waist, she pulled it out of his trousers, but Nick took over and lifted it over his head, flinging it to the floor.

"Are we even now?" he asked as he scooped her into his arms, against his bare chest, soaking up the softness of her curves.

"Not quite," Mercy told him as she kicked off her shoes and let her mouth retrace the steps his had taken earlier. She could taste the salt of his skin, and his nipple pebbled as she drew a circle around it with her tongue.

Nick groaned as he pushed her away. "Easy, *chère*. We're not half through, and you're trying to do me in."

While he took her mouth in another kiss, he undid her jeans, slipping a hand between the thin fabric of her panties and her belly. Knowing what he wanted and wanting it just as much, Mercy widened her stance, arching a bit into his searching fingers. When he found the curls at the apex of her thighs, a tiny moan began to form in the back of her throat.

As Nick brushed the soft bud of her womanhood, he swallowed her moan and let his fingers sink into her heat. Everything about her was soft and welcoming. She was as moist for him as he was hard for her. Reluctantly, he withdrew his hand and cupped her rump, guiding her to match his rhythm as he pressed his arousal against her.

Dieu, but he wanted this woman! Just touching her brought him close to the edge.

Mercy sensed the spiraling need in Nick that matched the rising desire she felt. When she freed his erection from the confines of his trousers, she was rewarded with an utterly masculine sound of satisfaction. His arousal pulsed beneath her fingers as she caressed him. Mercy reveled in the power she felt within her grasp and the urgency she could create with a few strokes.

"Mais non, chère," Nick told her, knowing that if he let her continue, he wouldn't be able to control his release. He wanted to complete what they had started, but he needed to be inside her, as deep as he could get. "If I'm going to finish, I'm going to finish inside you."

His blunt language sent a wave of excitement rolling through her, because she knew she'd brought him to this point. Stripping off the rest of their clothing and sheathing Nick's erection only took a moment, and then he pressed Mercy down onto the bed. He stroked and touched her, played with her until he felt her body begin to tense. Then he slid his knee between her thighs as he rose above her, urging her to open to him without words.

Nick caught his breath and paused as his hardness met her softness. With an effort that took all his concentration, he entered her slowly, creating a velvet torture for himself. All his self-control vanished when Mercy's inner muscles contracted around him and her hips rose to bring him completely inside her.

Together they found a hard rhythm that sent them rushing toward the finish. Every stroke felt more intimate and deeper than the last. Mercy's head twisted gently from side to side, and a soft cry tore from her throat as she reached for and caught the stars that exploded around her. Nick's own climax was wrung from him at the sound of her pleasure, leaving him spent and sated as he felt completion course through him in shock waves of satisfaction.

Nick gently transferred Mercy's sleeping body from his arms to the pillow and tucked the sheet around her. He tugged on his shorts and trousers before he quietly left the room. In her kitchen, he made some coffee, noting the fact that since the last time he'd rummaged around her pantry, she'd bought some chicory blend at a gourmet shop. Little by little he was becoming a part of her thoughts, and he liked that.

While the coffee brewed he studied the dawn as it crept through the branches of the huge crab-apple tree by the backyard fence. He felt a little like the dawn himself, sneaking up on Mercy's subconscious. Last night he'd made love to her a second time, as if the most intimate act between a man and a woman could bind her to him and make her forget whatever demons scared her away from love.

If nothing else, last night taught him that he wanted more than a place in Mercy's life. He wanted a place in her heart. Too bad the woman's heart lit up with a No Vacancy sign whenever a man got close. She guarded her heart the way that damn crab-apple tree guarded the fence. Somehow he'd have to find a way to slip in under her guard. He'd have to, because he wasn't going to give her up. If that meant backing off until she got used to the idea of loving him, then he'd try.

Mercy woke up, not because light filtered into the room announcing daybreak, but because she reached for and couldn't find Nick. Sitting upright, she smelled the coffee and saw his shoes and his purple polo shirt on the floor. Unfortunately, she didn't know whether she should be glad to find that Nick hadn't fled into the darkness after last night or appalled that he was such an early riser.

When she glanced at the alarm clock, she groaned and pulled the covers over her head, trying to go back to sleep. Anytime before seven o'clock was too early to rise by her standards. Too early to do anything! Especially on weekends. Especially on annoyingly quiet weekends like this one. She could hear the silence in the room; it was deafening. Resigned, Mercy uncovered her head and said, "If you're going to stick around, Dr. Devereaux, we're going to have to get a few ground rules straight."

As soon as she said it, Mercy clamped a hand over her mouth and bolted upright, clutching the covers to her. *Now you've done it. You're thinking in terms of Nick being a permanent fixture. Get a grip, Mercy May. What you had was great sex, not the beginning of something beautiful. You know what will happen if you allow yourself to get attached. You'll forget where his life ends and yours begins. "I" becomes "we," and when he's gone, you'll hurt like hell because you won't remember how to be alone.*

Dragging the sheet around her, Mercy got purposefully out of bed and crossed the room. She pulled clean underwear out of a drawer and grabbed the first top and pair of shorts her hands touched. Tiptoeing across the hallway, she locked herself in the bathroom to recover from the shock of having admitted, even to herself, that she wanted Nick to be more than a good time, more than a friend. Those were scary thoughts. How could she forget, even for a moment, the bitter fights and broken relationships that littered her childhood like Nick's clothes littered her floor?

Falling in love was like letting someone sink their teeth into your chest and standing idly by, waiting for them to rip your heart out. No, the life her parents had wasn't for her. *Then why are you hoping for more than last night?*

Mercy plucked her toothbrush out of the holder and tried to come up with an answer. Once her teeth sparkled, her face was scrubbed, and her hair brushed, she'd convinced herself that having more than a one-night stand with Nick wasn't the same thing as losing her heart to him. She could cut it off anytime she wanted, she promised herself as she stared into the medicine-cabinet mirror. "An affair is more than a good time and technically less than a serious relationship. Right? Right."

Ready to face Nick, Mercy left the bathroom. After all, why should she deny herself the pleasure of his company, in or out of bed, as long as he could be trusted to maintain the proper perspective. He seemed willing to do that. At the roadhouse, hadn't he promised he didn't want anything more than she was ready to give?

Her clever conscience waited until she was halfway down the stairs before reminding her that what Nick had actually said was he "wouldn't *take* anything more than she was *willing* to give." The man hadn't made any promises beyond that.

Obviously, he hadn't made any promises about being discreet either, since the front door stood wide open. Mercy suspected Nick was resting in the swing, barefoot and bare-chested for all the neighborhood to see. The man certainly had a flair for creating small-town gossip.

Mercy hesitated before walking onto the porch, afraid of what she might find. Having everything about last night analyzed, organized, and explained in her own mind didn't mean that Nick had come to the same conclusions. What if he wouldn't settle for an affair? What if he had that look, the one men got when they finally decided to make a monogamous commitment? What if he got all morning-after sappy and wanted promises she couldn't make?

She honestly didn't know what she'd say, because what she felt for Nick she'd never felt for anyone else. Friendship and passion were all mixed up with the fear of trusting him. Of trusting in love. Hadn't she seen marriage after marriage break up because somebody stopped caring? She reminded herself that the trick was not to care in the first place.

Steeling herself, she pushed open the screen. As it turned out, the first words out of Nick's mouth were far from morning-after sappy. They were downright rude and did more to put her at ease than anything he could have done.

TEN

"It lives, I see," Nick said, and saluted her with his coffee. He lowered his cup and added, "Barely."

"What's that supposed to mean?" she asked indignantly, all her concerns forgotten as she reached to take a sip of his coffee and plopped down beside him.

"It means you were dead to the world when I got up."

"Everybody was dead to the world when you got up," she pointed out testily.

"I wouldn't know about everybody. 'Cause I couldn't hear everybody else snoring."

"I don't snore!"

"I didn't say you did. I just said that I couldn't hear everybody else."

He grinned at her, and Mercy thought maybe, just maybe, falling into bed with Nick Devereaux hadn't been a mistake after all. Instead of looking for promises, he was looking for her sense of humor. Instead of crowding her this morning, he'd given her space. More importantly, instead of leaving, he'd parked his rump on her front porch, silently assuring her that he wanted more than last night but was willing to take everything one step at a time.

They swung in peace for a moment before they heard the argument between Sophie and Witch. Sophie won. Her neighbor refused to be dragged across the street at a breakneck pace and dug in her heels at the curb edge, sternly telling Witch to hold her horses. "Mercy! Send that young man of yours over here to get this dog before I say a few things to her that will make my pastor frown."

Knowing now was not the time to debate whether or not Nick was her "young man," Mercy simply waved and hollered, "Right away!"

"Throwing me to the wolves?" Nick asked as he got up and padded across the porch.

"Better you than me," she said right behind him. "Maybe she'll be too polite to ask you personal questions about why you're practically naked and sitting on my porch."

Nick paused at the edge of the steps to study the elderly woman who had managed to subdue Witch by having her lie down and then standing on the leash. Sophie waited with her arms akimbo and an expectant expression on her face. Shaking his head, Nick said, "Don't fool yourself. Sophie would ask personal questions of the pope without blinking an eye."

Pushing him from behind, Mercy said, "Just remember. Only name, rank, and serial number." She stopped him by placing a hand on his biceps to whisper, "But don't be abrupt. Be casual, or she'll smell a secret. Talk about gardening or the weather."

"Only name, rank, and serial number," Nick repeated as he walked through the yard. Since Sophie had begun tapping her foot at his leisurely pace, he loped across the asphalt street and held out his hand for the leash.

Instead of the lead, Sophie handed him a conversational hot potato. "I see you've made some progress with our Mercy since that picnic."

"Yes, ma'am. Considerable." Nick continued to hold out his hand as he repeated to himself, name, rank, and serial number.

"Well," Sophie huffed as she slapped the leather strap into his palm and stepped away from the Labrador. "With that attitude you're not likely to make any more progress, are you?"

Surprised, Nick gave the older woman a hard stare, and Mercy's advice was completely forgotten. "Exactly what are you trying to tell me, Sophie?"

"Mercy's a healthy, red-blooded, American girl."

Looking back over his shoulder, Nick had to agree. She was wearing the same outfit she'd worn the first time he met her—old, faded cutoffs and a little scrap of a white top. From where he was standing, Mercy definitely looked all-American—all legs and curves and memories of last night. Then his attention swiveled back to Sophie, who waited patiently and looked a bit smug.

"Mercy is all of those things and more," he told her. "So what's your point?"

"You've won a tiny battle, not the war." Sophie smoothed back some silver hair with short broad fingers; the gesture unconsciously betrayed her uncertainty about how she wanted to approach the subject at hand. "Spending the night doesn't constitute considerable progress. That girl ... You're not ..."

As she hesitated, obviously searching for words, a grin tugged at the corners of Nick's mouth. "Don't spare my feelings, Sophie. I might like my whiskey with Coke, but I like my truth straight up."

"Well, to be perfectly blunt, Mercy's not going to change her mind about marriage because Nick Devereaux spent the night."

"Who said anything about marriage?"

A peal of laughter broke from Sophie. "Don't kid a kidder, son. If you were only interested in the bedroom, then why did you announce your intentions to the entire neighborhood by planting yourself on that front porch like you'd come to stay?"

"Is that what I did?"

"That's exactly what you did. I knew you had marriage on your mind when I saw the look on your face at the Fourth of July picnic. You looked like you'd been kicked in the head by a mule. I thought to myself, Now there's a man our Mercy won't be able to scare off. You're head over heels for the girl, so let's not waste time arguing about something we both know is true."

Nick mulled that over while he scratched Witch behind the ears. "I didn't realize it was quite so obvious. Thanks for the warning. I'll keep it in mind. And thanks for keeping Witch." Mercy hovered anxiously on the porch, so he smiled to let her know that everything was fine and patted his leg for Witch to get up. "Let's go, girl."

"I've met her parents, you know," Sophie said casually as he stepped off the curb. "Both of them."

A simple sentence, but one that stopped Nick cold. He glanced back at Sophie, all the while trying to look casual so Mercy wouldn't think she needed to dash over and rescue him. As easily as he could, he stopped the dog and prompted Sophie at the same time. "And?"

"I don't believe I've ever met two more self-absorbed people as those knife-happy doctors. All they can talk about is procedures and who's been asked to speak where. Can't imagine how Mercy managed to turn out so well having to grow up with those two egomaniacs as examples. It's a pity, really."

"Sounds like it," Nick said in the kind of voice that was meant to encourage Sophie's observations.

"A real pity for that girl. Growing up with the kind of people who like to blame their troubles on everyone but themselves." Sophie put her hands on her thin hips and rolled her eyes. "And the way those two get married, there's always a convenient new victim to blame for their desperate unhappiness."

"You mean when the relationship falls apart?"

"Of course. It's inevitable."

"Inevitable?" Nick prodded.

"Those two probably couldn't hold a marriage together with a gallon of Super Glue even if their lives depended on it. But why should they bother trying? There's always Mercy to pick up the pieces. To listen to their sad tales of woe and heartache. Always Mercy who holds their hands until they find a new victim who makes them feel exciting and happy for a while."

Suddenly everything clicked into place for him.

Mercy had given up being happy so she could avoid being unhappy. She wasn't scared of commitment. She was scared of love, scared it wouldn't last. She was more scared of being hurt than she was of being alone.

"Remind me to send you roses, Sophie."

"What you can send me is an invitation."

"To the benefit? You got it."

Sophie rolled her eyes and shook her head. "I can see I'm going to have to be plain. I'm a lonely old woman since Art passed on last year. We never had children, so I've gotten in the habit of pretending that Mercy is mine. I'd like to see that girl walk down the aisle before I'm done, and you're the first genuine prospect I've had. Don't blow it."

Nick made a show of adjusting Witch's collar as he said, "I don't suppose you'd mind bouncing a a grandbaby or two before you're done?"

Beaming, Sophie said, "I believe we understand one another."

"Yes, ma'am. I believe we do."

Sunday morning Mercy kissed Nick good-bye and shut the door. Smiling confidently at Witch, she said, "See how easy that is? A couple of great nights and now it's back to normal. No muss. No fuss. I don't know why I didn't think of this before."

Witch barked and wagged.

"You're damn right. We can cut it off anytime we want. Just 'cause I sleep with him doesn't mean I have to sleep with him all the time. We don't need some man cluttering up the house." Mercy headed for the kitchen and leftovers. "Although this one can really cook."

"What are you doing here?" Mercy asked in exasperation when she opened the door Monday morning. How was she going to run this affair according to her timetable if he was going to show up anytime he felt like it?

"Ah, *chère*, someone's got to fix the back-fence gate before it falls off the hinges."

"That someone doesn't have to be you," she told him firmly, making a point of not opening the screen.

"You gonna do it?"

"Eventually!"

"Right. You got a jigsaw to trim off the bottom of the gate where it's dragging? A circular saw? Any kind of saw for that matter?"

Mercy wanted to shut the door in his face, but the truth was, she had missed him, even though a mere twenty-four hours shouldn't be enough time to miss anybody. "Okay, Mr. Fix-It, what's it going to cost me?"

"Nothing."

Mercy blanched and clutched a hand to her breast dramatically. "Oh, my word! That much? Please. I'd rather pay than owe you."

"Darlin', I'd rather you owe me."

"I'll just bet you would." Giving in, Mercy said, "Come in, but don't expect me to entertain you or go to the hardware store. I've got work to do. You'll just have to make yourself at home."

"Believe me, *chère*, I intend to," Nick murmured

as he gave her a kiss and then headed for the back, toolbox in hand.

"That's what I'm afraid of," Mercy whispered when he disappeared into the dining room. "And once you do, I'm afraid I'll get used to having you around."

By the weekend, Mercy found herself thinking in terms of "when Nick gets home" instead of "the next time I see Nick." That stopped her cold, until she rationalized that the amount of time they spent together didn't matter as long as she remembered the arrangement was temporary. She hadn't done anything stupid yet. She hadn't *officially* asked him to move in. She hadn't vowed eternal love. She was safe. As safe as a girl could be around Nick Devereaux.

In the wee hours of the morning, Mercy turned over to snuggle closer to Nick, who slept peacefully beside her and adjusted for her body, never waking. Mercy smiled, knowing it must be raining. Nick actually slept when it rained, real sleep, restful sleep. Contentedly, Mercy closed her eyes, intending to drift back to sleep until she realized that it wasn't raining. Not a drop. She stayed awake the rest of the night guarding his sleep and feeling incredibly powerful. The man who didn't sleep was sleeping in her bed. She felt as if she'd been given an incredible gift.

As D day approached, Witch got rounder and rounder. Mercy and Nick placed bets on exactly when she'd explode. Between their schedules, they made sure one of them was at home all the time during the last few days. Just in case.

Freshly showered, Nick leaned on the door facing Mercy's living room, noting the subtle changes that had taken place in his life during the last two weeks. For one thing, his apartment was nothing more than a place to hang his hat now that an antiquated house in Haunt, Kentucky, was home. His collection of tools was growing in direct proportion to the number of fix-it-yourself projects he had completed, and a few of his old jerseys had somehow found their way into Mercy's possession.

The gold-colored jersey she wore at the moment said GATOR BAIT in deep green letters on the front and BAYOU GRILL in blood red on the back.

There were other changes too. Like becoming a pseudo-father. After pacing nervously for the better part of two days, Witch had finally delivered her puppies. Most of the furniture had been shoved back to make room for a large whelping box, from which incredibly loud suckling noises were emanating.

Mercy, wearing only his shirt, perched on the edge of the sheet-covered navy-striped sofa as she leaned over to peek at the nine, newly arrived, plump black puppies. Occasionally, the contented suckling noises were interrupted by a complaint from a disgruntled puppy who'd fallen off a nipple and couldn't find it again. Cocking his head to listen more closely, Nick could hear a faint umm-umm-umm noise escalating from a grunt to a cry. Efficiently, Mercy reached over the box and pointed the wailing puppy in the proper direction.

Mercy was an authority on the latest in accepted canine delivery procedures. At least on paper. However, Nick handled the actual whelping, due to his previous experience in delivering babies. Not that his experience stopped Mercy from hovering nervously during the whole process, offering advice, and reading aloud from what seemed like an endless supply of books on how to whelp puppies.

Finally, Nick had had to sit her down and tell her point-blank that she was beginning to make Witch nervous. He'd heard couples say that if you could survive wallpapering without killing each other, then nothing could tear you apart. Nick thought whelping puppies was right up there with wallpapering as the acid test of a relationship.

Once the puppies had arrived, he'd barely been able to talk Mercy into leaving them long enough to shower. Right now, as she watched mother and puppies resting peacefully, Mercy's expression was positively maternal. Nick thought the expression looked good on her. As he pushed away from the frame he asked, "I thought I'd find you here. Are you gonna to sit there all day?"

Noticing him, Mercy smiled and crooked her finger. "They've gained weight just in the time we've been gone. I swear. Come see." Mercy patted the sofa before gazing back down at the puppies. "Mother Nature sure knew what she was doing with this baby business."

"I thought one of your rules was no children."

Mercy looked up, startled. "I never said that. As I recall, that was one of your sweeping assumptions."

"So, children are okay with you?" Nick queried, an odd light in his dark eyes.

"Yes. Why?" she asked suspiciously.

"Curiosity."

"Killed the cat," she told him.

Planting a firm kiss on her mouth, Nick slid down on the sofa and told her, "If I'm going to die, then I have to know one more thing."

"What's that?"

"Do you put on a bra with that tux jacket you're so fond of wearing on the show? The one that's cut down to here." He touched her abdomen in the general vicinity of her belly button.

She primly swatted his hand away while getting up. "My tux jacket is not cut down to there. You know, Nick, you seem to have this thing about women's underwear."

"Only yours, *chère*. Only yours." With a quick tug, Nick pulled her off balance, tumbled her back onto the sofa, her legs landing in his lap and her rump on the cushion beside him. Nick fingered the edge of the gold jersey before he slipped his hand beneath it. "And right now, yours is in my way."

Mercy caught her breath as his hand curled around the elastic of her panties and pulled them down until she could kick them off. The instant softening she felt every time Nick touched her continued to surprise her. Never in her life had she melted simply because a man touched her.

With calculated slowness, his index finger toyed with the inside of her knee. He could see the muscles in her neck contract as she swallowed. Her thighs parted a fraction of an inch in silent entreaty. Catching and holding her gaze, Nick moved his hand higher on her thigh, toward the soft, dark curls barely revealed by the upturned edge of the jersey. When his fingers pushed through the curls and splayed against her belly, Mercy closed her eyes with a ragged sigh.

Wanting Nick this much had to be crazy, she told herself, but she couldn't manage to care. Instead, she slid a leg off his lap and opened her body to him, trusting him to know what she needed. As she opened, the pad of his thumb found the center of her desire, manipulating it and creating tiny pulses of pleasure designed to drive her mad. Too soon her hips were lifting gently with the rhythm of his stokes, and she knew she needed more. She needed the inexplicable satisfaction she got when her body and soul were fused with Nick's.

Watching Mercy writhe beneath his touch was incendiary to Nick's passion. When her back arched, he pulled her up, his pants already open and his arousal free. Mercy straddled his hips, her mouth slightly open as she lowered herself to complete the union.

Nick shuddered and tried to hold her there by resting the palms of his hands on her hips and molding his fingers around her silky bottom, but she wouldn't stay still. She squirmed beneath his fingertips, breaking his hold and rising until she held only the tip of his erection inside her, teasing him with tiny plunges that engulfed the tip and inflamed him further. Giving in, Nick pulled her down roughly as he thrust into her, repeating the action again and again until he knew he'd explode.

Always lost in his arms, Mercy began to quiver.

Heat coiled in her womb, threatening to spill through her body, and when it did, she grabbed onto Nick and held tight. A second later she felt him shudder and heard him whisper hoarsely, *"Bon Dieu. Merci Dieu!"* as the pleasure claimed him too.

Nick stood outside the door of the complimentary suite the hotel had given Mercy for the evening and remembered the last time he'd gone knocking on a strange door looking for Midnight Mercy. Bracing himself, he waited for her. When she opened the door, his heart actually stopped as something one of the paramedics said came back to him. Nick couldn't take his eyes off her. He whispered, "Have mercy on my soul."

Normally spectacular, Mercy's body defied description in the curve-hugging dress of dripping black icicles she wore. Miles of leg showed, and the slightest movement made the covering of icicles shimmer like black ice. The only thing remotely demure about the gown was the abbreviated turtleneck collar, which actually served to accentuate her breasts while baring her shoulders and arms completely.

When she turned to pick up a matching evening bag, Nick cursed. The damn dress was backless. Russet hair rippled and tumbled partway down, but not far enough to reach the sweet spot at the small of her back. Before he recovered from the first shock, he got another. Hell, the dress was practically bottomless too! The hanging icicles made it appear to cover more thigh than the dress really did.

Nick tugged at his stiff collar. Tonight was going

to be a long night. Midnight and the end of Ghouls' Nite Out couldn't come a minute too soon as far as he was concerned.

"Well," Mercy said once she had her purse in her hand. "Either you love it or hate it. Which is it?"

"Both."

Laughing, Mercy closed the door and slipped her arm through his. "I could say the same about you. That's a pretty snazzy European tux you've got on."

"I'm only following orders. My invitation said black tie and black stalkings."

"How odd," Mercy puzzled as she pushed the elevator button. "I must have read it too quickly. I thought the invitation said black tie and black *stockings*. How silly of me. I even dug out my one and only garter belt for the occasion."

Before Nick could muster a reply, the elevator opened. The people inside recognized her instantly. As she chatted amiably with her public Nick was left to stew in the fantasies created by the woman beside him.

Twenty minutes later the hotel staff dimmed the lights, and Nick surveyed the prefunction area outside the larger banquet room. Mercy was in constant demand for autographs as she moved through the crowd. Judging from the number of heads whipping around to stare as she walked toward him, Nick would have bet that her dress was the subject of more than one conversation around the room. And rightfully so. The woman could drive a man to drink.

"*Laissez les bons temps rouler*," Nick said, raising his

glass of chardonnay as she approached. "Let the good times roll."

"That's easy for you to say," Mercy told him flippantly. "You're not waiting for my parents to walk in and cast a pall over the evening."

"Of course I am, *chère*. I'm on pins and needles waiting for them to ask me what my intentions are toward their lovely daughter."

"If I were you, I wouldn't worry too much. At this point, chances are less than fifty–fifty that they'll show up to ask you anything."

"They'll show, *chère*. Else they would've called."

"No, I'm afraid that's not how it works in my family." More resigned than sad, Mercy finally faced the fact that she'd never be more than an afterthought in her parents' lives. To be perfectly honest, tonight the only face in the crowd she'd tried to find had been Nick's. He always seemed to know, and he'd turn his head toward her, sharing the moment and a smile.

Standing next to Nick reminded her that people worth caring about also knew how to care about others. Maybe she was in the market for a man to clutter up her life after all. She walked her fingernails up his lapel. "I can ask you about your intentions toward me if you're just dying to tell someone."

"Too late. Sophie already asked."

"And what did you tell her?"

"Nothing she didn't already know," Nick assured her.

Mercy thumped him on the chest, irritated with his answer. "Well, you were sitting on my porch half-naked. What was she supposed to think?"

"I don't think it was my lack of shirt that gave

Sophie her ideas. She said it was the look on my face."

"You smirked, didn't you?"

"Not that I recall. Sophie said I looked like I'd been kicked in the head by a mule."

When Mercy's mouth dropped open, Nick reached over and closed it. "Pull yourself together, *chère*. Unless I'm totally mistaken about the resemblance, your mother has made her entrance."

Mercy whirled. Black icicles flicked rapid fire against Nick's tux as she turned. Her mother stood alone and observed the crowd like a lazy lioness who was confident of her ability to cut out the weak member of a herd. Raising her hand in a wave, Mercy said to Nick, "Hold on to your hat. Another one bit the dust."

"Excuse me?"

"Mother never goes anywhere alone. She chooses men on the basis of their willingness to escort her at the drop of a hat. If Vaughn isn't with her, I guarantee you, there is trouble in paradise."

"Thank the dear Lord that you're smarter than she is."

"About what?"

As her mother came toward them Nick whispered, "Choosing men."

"Mercy! You should thank me for passing on my figure and cheekbones. They look lovely on you."

Nick stiffened beside her, and Mercy had to suppress a smile. Meeting her mother was a shock. Even her compliments were self-serving. "Mother. I'd like to introduce you Dr. Nick Devereaux. Nick this is my mother, Dr. Alexandra Stanton."

"It's a pleasure to meet you, Doctor," she said graciously, and offered her hand briefly. "Your specialty?"

"Emergency. Mercy Hospital."

"Ah . . ." The word was dismissive, as if she found his specialty unworthy of conversation. Turning back to Mercy, she said, "Now, where is that young man you wanted me to meet. Don't tell me he's left you already?" She paused almost long enough for Mercy to answer, but not quite. "Vaughn and I are postponing the wedding, you know. Things aren't . . . going well."

For a moment Mercy was suckered by the hint of sadness in her mother's eyes and the regret in her voice, but before she could express her sympathy, her mother snapped to attention, all emotion vanished. "Lord, there's Hank! I'll be right back. I've got a case I'd like to discuss with him. Dr. Devereaux, would you like to join me? No?" As an afterthought, she glanced over her shoulder and said, "Save me a seat at dinner, Mercy. I'll meet the young man then."

"Slam, bam, thank you, ma'am," Nick uttered with a thunderstruck look on his face. "*Dieu.* Is she always like this?"

Mercy shook her head. "No. Often she's worse. At least she remembered I had someone I wanted her to meet even if she didn't remember the name."

"No wonder the woman can't keep a relationship together. She wouldn't know an honest, caring emotion if it bit her on the butt—" Nick winced, realizing how rude he sounded. "Sorry. She's your mother. I shouldn't have said anything."

She didn't answer for a long time, instead watching her mother eagerly talk shop across the room. In the blink of an eye Alexandra could relegate her personal life to second place and concentrate on medicine. The only thing she really cared about. The only thing that had been able to hold her interest over the years.

"Don't apologize, Nick. You're right. About everything. Mother doesn't choose well. She hasn't a clue what to look for or how to take care of it when she finds it."

Nick cupped the back of her neck with his hand and let his thumb stroke her skin. "You must have gotten all your warmth from your father."

Softly, Mercy said, "What father? The one that isn't here?"

"I'm here."

"I'm glad." Mercy smiled brightly, realizing that in the last few weeks she'd learned to trust him, to believe in what she saw every day. He cared about people, not just medicine.

After dinner, Mercy took the stage to thank everyone involved and announced the name of the lucky guest who'd been selected to cohost *The Midnight Hour*. Once all the commotion subsided, she had intended to deliver a brief dignified speech to reveal that they'd raised almost three hundred thousand dollars after expenses. But when she called Nick on stage to represent the hospital, a couple of the women in the crowd recognized him from the promos and soon had everyone hollering for Nick to kiss her again.

Astounded by the reaction, Mercy tried to control

her laughter. Roars of approval greeted Nick as he played to the crowd by bending Mercy backward in a re-creation of their promo kiss. From that point on, Mercy forgot about everything but Nick. If two thousand people thought they belonged together, who was she to argue?

Later, in the hotel suite, Mercy forgot everything but the feel of Nick's body as he covered her, loving her. Nick felt her complete surrender as their passion crested and she clung to him whispering his name as though she'd never let him go.

Easing away from her, Nick lay back against the pillows and cradled her head against his shoulder. Little by little he'd come alive again with Mercy. There wasn't a doubt about it anymore, Nick told himself. He had marriage on his mind. He wanted to see a ring on her finger and know that he had family again.

"We've reached a crossroads, *chère*. One of us is going to have to say it first. And I'm willing."

"To say what first?" Mercy murmured sleepily as she snuggled closer to his warmth, dropping a kiss on his chest.

"I love you."

ELEVEN

She stilled immediately, wide-awake, holding her breath, and afraid she'd heard him wrong. "Excuse me?"

"I . . . love . . . you."

Mercy pulled out of his arms, dragging the sheet around her and the hair out of her eyes as she searched his face. She wasn't ready for this. The whole idea of loving Nick, of wanting him as a permanent part of her life, was barely a few hours old. She wasn't sure she was prepared to say the words.

"Ah, *chère*." Nick shook his head at the stunned and uncertain look on her face. "Do you want me to engrave it in stone before you'll believe it?"

"It'd be a start at least," Mercy told him softly.

Her answer struck him as funny, and he laughed incredulously. "And what else would you like? I'll engrave it in a wedding band, spell it out with rocks, and write it in the sky, if you want."

"What I want is exactly what scares me," Mercy told him. "God knows I want to believe you."

"Then believe me. Let me inside your heart, Mercy. All the way this time."

Now it was Mercy's turn to laugh. "There isn't a woman alive who could keep you out, Nick Devereaux."

Nick snatched the sheet away and rolled her beneath him. "Does that mean you love me?"

"It must," whispered Mercy, admitting the truth. "Because I've never really tried to keep you out."

Nick's lips came down on hers, at once promising and demanding promises. Before Mercy could do more than wrap her arms around his neck, the telephone interrupted them.

"Don't answer it," Nick told her, working his way down her neck.

"We have to. It might be for you. Might be an emergency."

"It might be Publishers Clearing House with my million dollars, but I don't care."

Ignoring him, Mercy wiggled and stretched until she could reach the phone. "Hello? Just a minute." She covered the receiver. "Would you *stop* that. It's for you."

Annoyed, he lifted his mouth from paying homage to one rosy nipple and grabbed the telephone. "Devereaux. And this better be good."

While he listened to the voice on the phone, Mercy slipped on a robe and hugged the knowledge of his love close. Something she'd never dreamed possible had finally happened. She'd found someone she could trust with her heart. Wonders never ceased, because he was a doctor to boot.

Suddenly very still, Nick said, "I'll be right there. Give me about fifteen minutes." He let the receiver slide down his chest and then hung it up.

Children and teenagers were always the toughest for him, because he wanted to care more than he should. Lately, pushing back thoughts of Catherine lying helpless in an emergency room took every ounce of willpower he had. With an effort, he locked away his feelings and prepared himself to face what lay ahead. "I've got to go to the hospital."

"What's wrong?" she asked, aware of the controlled quality of his voice and the emotional distance created by Nick's sudden aloofness.

"An eighteen-wheeler plowed through the railing of an expressway overpass and crushed a busload of teenagers coming back from band camp. They're kids from the hospital neighborhood." He paused long enough to reach for his clothes lying at the foot of the bed. As he pulled on his pants he told her, "The regional trauma center's going to have more than it can handle once they start pulling bodies out of the wreckage. We're the closest hospital, so we'll be getting the overflow."

"How many? Did they say?"

Without so much as a look in her direction, Nick gave his tux shirt a good shake and slid into it. "Paramedics told the hospital to figure that as many as ten were coming our way. Some with serious injuries."

"But you're not equipped or staffed for something like this! You said so yourself. How are you going to handle so many cases?"

"Triage," he told her absently, his mind already

going over details he'd have to handle once he got to the hospital.

"Triage?"

"It's a protocol for treating the most seriously injured first." Nick finished buttoning his shirt, the adrenaline beginning to flow as he focused on the task ahead. "Even then, we may have to make hard choices. If I can save three lives, with the same resources it would take to save one, I've got to save three. Or risk losing all four." He scanned the floor. "Have you seen my shoes?"

Mercy didn't answer. She was remembering her first tour of the emergency room, how he'd disconnected his emotions and become all doctor, all business, just like her parents. "You really are prepared to make choices like that," Mercy whispered, cold fingers closing around her heart. "You can decide who to help."

"It's a matter of priorities. You gotta make a decision and move on."

Priorities? Move on?

How could the warm, caring man who shared her bed moments before turn off his emotions like that? She didn't know the dispassionate and detached man standing in front of her. How could Nick talk about protocols and priorities instead of worrying about people and pain? How could he divorce himself so totally from his emotions that he could accept the loss of one patient and walk calmly to the next based on *priorities*?

Until this moment she hadn't wanted to believe he could be cold and unfeeling like her parents. She'd fooled herself into believing that he was different. But he wasn't different; he didn't care about people. He cared about the high he got from playing God. She wasn't any better at choosing men than her mother.

"I gotta go, *chère*. I'll call you when I'm done." His brief kiss good-bye felt mechanical, almost like an afterthought.

When the door shut behind him, Mercy let the tears roll down her cheeks. She'd been a fool for ignoring the other side of Nick, the side she'd seen during the hospital tour. She'd been an even bigger fool for believing she could spend so much time with him and not fall in love.

"Dear God in heaven," Mercy whispered as she rocked, hugging a pillow to her midriff. "If he can decide when to care, if he can turn it on and off, what's to say he won't stop loving me when it's no longer convenient?"

How can you love a man you can never be sure of?

"How do I *stop* loving him?" She threw the pillow across the bed.

She'd ignored all her rules, and now she had to pay the price. Nick might be able to flip his emotions on and off like a switch, but she couldn't. She couldn't stop loving him, but neither would she spend every day waiting for the other shoe to drop, waiting for him to flip a switch and forget why he loved her. The longer she waited, the more it was going to hurt. She had to cut it off now, before it got any worse. Before she gave him an even bigger piece of her heart to break.

Making up her mind, Mercy knew she'd have to tell Nick she'd mistaken her feelings. Now that the benefit was over, everything could go back to the way it was before he showed up on her porch. She didn't need Nick; she never had to see him again after she said good-bye. All she needed was her life back and the hurt to go away.

All she needed was to get somewhere safe, like home.

Suddenly she realized that even going home would hurt. Reminders of Nick were everywhere—the shiny red toolbox in the front closet; chicory coffee in the pantry; cloves of garlic in a hanging basket in the kitchen window; a soft, well-worn jersey that smelled like him; a spare toothbrush in the bathroom. Even the sound of the rain against the windows would remind her of him.

Little by little Nick had crept into her life and into her soul. She couldn't say he hadn't warned her about broken hearts. He had. He'd said when a woman got her heart broken, she knew who and where and when. He was right.

For the first time in a long time, tears pricked Nick's eyes, and he needed a minute to compose himself before he walked into the waiting room. Nine patients had come through the hospital doors. Only eight of them were still alive. The last kid—Tommy—had fought every inch of the way, and so had Nick. But now all that was left of Tommy was memories.

Because of Catherine, he had insulated himself from becoming too attached to the people he treated. He hadn't allowed himself to hurt this much in a long time. Now all he wanted to do was curl up beside the woman he loved and forget that his best hadn't been good enough to save a thirteen-year-old kid—a kid whose only request had been that they not lose his first-place band-camp ribbon as they cut off his shirt.

How did he tell two loving parents that his best hadn't been good enough to save their child? How could he possibly hope to make this easier on them? By pretending to be steady and calm? By throwing technical jargon at them to discourage them from asking questions about how their son faced death?

Non. Not anymore.

Swinging around, Nick made a decision and retrieved the ribbon from the treatment room. He was through pretending he didn't care. It didn't make him hurt any less. It didn't take away the fear that Catherine had died alone in a cold room surrounded by strangers. He would have given the world to know that someone held Catherine's hand at the end. That someone had cared enough to fight like hell for her.

Tommy's parents were going to know that. They were going to know the courage their son had possessed, how he had hung on to life. They were going to know that he hadn't died among strangers—even if telling them opened up his old wounds. It was time to let go of the past.

Nick inserted the card-style key and opened the hotel-suite door. As soon as he tiptoed into the bedroom, he realized his efforts to be considerate were wasted. The bed was empty. Tapping on the closed bathroom door, he said, "I'm back."

When she didn't answer, Nick tapped louder.

"You in there, *chère*?" Frowning, he called, "Mercy? I'm comin' in."

The cavernous lavatory was not only empty, it was also spick-and-span. Not so much as a washcloth had been used. Nick's eyebrows lifted in surprise. Mercy had made her feelings about crawling out of bed at the crack of dawn very clear. She didn't get up before seven, and yet she was already up and gone.

Walking back to the bed, Nick picked up the phone and rang the front desk. "This is Nick Devereaux in Room 910. Did someone leave a message for me? No? Thanks."

Without waiting, Nick depressed the hook, then dialed again. This time he keyed in Mercy's home number. He let it ring fifteen times before he hung up. Then he dialed Sophie, who told him that yes, Mercy had made it home safely about five o'clock in the morning; no, she didn't think anything was wrong with the phone; and yes, she'd keep an eye on Mercy.

Thoughtful, Nick thanked her and returned the receiver to the cradle. Mercy hadn't left a message and wasn't answering the phone. Surely she wasn't upset about his going to the hospital in an emergency. After all, she was the one who'd answered the phone. What in hell bothered her so much that she felt she had to go home without saying a word? He swore softly and tried to remember everything that happened from the moment the hospital called.

Bon Dieu! He'd just gotten through telling her how much he loved her! And she loved him! Not that she'd actually said the words, but the sentiment was implicit in how she responded to him. How could one phone call change all that?

Concentrating, he put his head in his hands and went back over their conversation. He told her about the accident. They talked about how many cases the hospital was expecting. She worried about how they could handle that many. He told her about triage, and—Nick's head snapped up as he remembered a quiet comment.

You really are prepared to make choices like that.

He hadn't explained how difficult the choices sometimes were, or how little time the staff had to evaluate patients when lives hung in the balance. He hadn't told her that having to live with the decisions was his own personal nightmare. He hadn't told her that he pretended not to care so he didn't think about Catherine being alone and dying.

Non. He hadn't told her any of that. What had he done instead?

The memory of his answer tasted bitter in his mouth. He'd assured her he could make that choice. He'd told her it was a matter of priorities, of making a medical decision and getting on with it. In short, he'd told her he was a cold-blooded, emotionless machine. Everything she was afraid of.

"Ah, *chère,* how we gonna get anywhere if you keep running away?"

Maybe it was time he told her about Catherine. Starting out for Haunt, Kentucky, Nick only stopped long enough to toss his key to a clerk at the front desk.

The rumble of Nick's car engine sounded angry to Mercy as she sat on the sofa by the whelping box.

Apprehensive, she got up and went to unlock the door, knowing that there would never be a "good" time for her to face Nick. She didn't imagine that coming back to an empty hotel room put him in a terrific frame of mind—not to mention that he hadn't been to sleep in more than twenty-four hours. Until this moment she hadn't realized how much she'd been counting on his exhaustion to buy her some time, but it seemed her time had just run out.

As she reached for the lock a subtle irony occurred to her. In the last few weeks she'd given him the key to her heart, but never got around to giving him a key to the door. If she'd been smart, she would have done it the other way around. A lock was a lot easier to change than her heart. Bracing herself, she pulled open the door and was struck by a feeling of déjà vu.

A gorgeous man stood on her porch, pulled off his sunglasses, and their eyes met. His were shadowed and tired, just like they had been before. Only this time she knew why he hadn't gotten much sleep.

Unable to stop the knee-jerk reaction of concern, she told him, "You're dead on your feet. You shouldn't have driven all the way out here."

"I wouldn't have had to if you'd picked up the phone." When she didn't say anything or open the screen door, Nick swore in French and said softly, "Ah, *chère*, we gonna do this the hard way, or you gonna tell me straight up what'sa matter?"

Mercy didn't give up her position in the doorway, blocking his passage.

"*Non?* You gonna make me stand out here on the porch and guess?"

Before she answered, she warned herself that appearances were deceiving. Nick might look concerned; he might say all the right words, but she knew better than to trust him. He'd given her a perfect demonstration of his ability to make a one-hundred-and-eighty-degree turn in the emotion department. "I was going to call you."

"When? Tomorrow? Next week? Not good enough!" Nick had to remind himself that Mercy didn't know how to fight for a relationship. She'd never had any practice, and her parents sure as hell hadn't taught her. Calmly, he put his sunglasses in his pocket and got a grip on his temper.

"Why'd you leave the hotel, Mercy? Is this some sort of test to see if I would even notice? To see if I'd come after you? Are you such a coward that you're gonna waste all your time measuring my commitment instead of enjoying what we have?"

Mercy stiffened. He was back to calling her a coward again, but this time she didn't take the bait. This wasn't about losing her nerve. This was about trusting Nick, and she couldn't do that anymore. "What do we have? Really? We have some good nights and a few laughs. That's all. What did you think we had?"

Nick was stunned. He rested his hands on his hips and said, "Some good nights and a few laughs were obviously a helluva lot more precious to me than you. I thought we were on the way to making a life together."

Looking away for a moment, Mercy had to steel herself against the passion and conviction she heard in his voice as he talked about a life together. He made it sound so real. Her heart wanted to believe him, but she knew better. She'd seen him go cold. "You thought wrong. We never made each other any promises."

The expression on Nick's face called her a liar. "If we weren't making a life, then what we had, *chère*, was an emotional chicken game. And darlin', you drove off the road first. I didn't. I'm still here."

"But for how long?" she whispered before she could stop herself.

Nick wondered if she realized what she'd said, how much she'd exposed to him about her fears. He wondered if she truly knew how much he needed her, or even how much he loved her. Softly, he said, "I'm not going anywhere, *chère*."

She almost believed him, and then she remembered how easy it was to believe what you wanted to believe. Her mother always did. That's why she made such bad choices. She always saw what she wanted to see. Shaking her head, she said, "Whether or not you're going anywhere doesn't matter."

"The hell it doesn't," Nick told her hotly. He wasn't about to let her pretend not to care. He knew all about pretending. It didn't help. It didn't make the hurt go away. It didn't make everything all right.

Mercy forced herself to meet his gaze, which scorched her despite the wire screen between them. "Don't make this difficult, Nick. Last night was my wake-up call. I realized that I let this relationship get out of hand. I made a mistake."

"*Mais yeah!* You made a mistake all right. You fell in love with a man who loves you back." The intensity in his eyes underscored the passion in his declaration.

Her bottom lip quivered for a minute and her resolve wavered, but she pulled it together before a single tear escaped. She couldn't trust him, not for always. She couldn't forget that. "I didn't fall in love. I fell in lust. Call it temporary insanity. I got real life confused with Midnight Mercy. It's the only possible explanation for why an intelligent woman managed to forget every principle of her existence. I didn't mean to fall into a relationship with you."

"You didn't mean to? *You didn't mean to?*"

Nick was through waiting for an invitation. He flung open the screen door so hard that it hit the house and the old spring snapped. After a bounce, the door stayed wide open, and Nick tried to get a handle on his temper. Mercy was right in front of him, and he so badly wanted to make her tell him the truth so they could deal with it out in the open.

"If I walk away right now, what are you gonna do, Mercy? Go back to the way you were—adopting furniture instead of having a family of your own? Picking up the pieces of your parents' lives when they remember you're alive?"

"It's better than picking up the pieces of my life." She stood her ground and held his gaze, daring him to argue and hoping to God he would, telling herself that he couldn't be that angry if he didn't really care.

"*Dieu*, Mercy! You don't throw away something precious because you think it's broken or might break. You fix it and make it stronger. Don't you get it? A relationship is just like this house. You don't go out and buy everything new when something goes wrong. You fix it. *We* can fix it." He walked into the entrance hall and kicked the door shut behind him. "Whatever's wrong, we can fix it. Together, Mercy. Together."

A tear threatened until she tilted her head back and took a deep breath. She backed away from him. It was either that or risk melting into his arms and ruining her chance to make a clean break of it. "The difference between what we have and this house is that this house is at least standing on a solid foundation."

"Why are you so afraid to believe in us?"

"I'm afraid because we jumped into this relationship without looking where we were going. We're standing in a swamp and up to our ass in alligators! And I don't have to be bitten before I know it's time to move on!"

"No gain, no pain," he murmured as he walked toward her. "Is that it? Are we back to that?"

"No, that's not it! This isn't just about me. It's about you."

"Then help me understand why you walked out!" He grabbed her arms and pulled her to his chest. "You owe me that. Say it, Mercy. Tell me why you're afraid of loving me."

"Because someday you're going to flip the switch on your personal emotions exactly like you do in the emergency room," she yelled at him, hurt, angry, and scared. All of those feelings made her cry, and in combination they were deadly. She gave up and let the tears flow as she whispered, "Someday you're going to stop caring, and there isn't a damn thing I can do about it."

"Yes. There is." Gently, he reached out and curved

his palm along her jaw and rubbed a tear away with his thumb. The hard part was over. For her anyway. She'd said the words. She'd gotten her fear out. Now it was up to him to make her believe. The only way to do that was to tell her the truth.

"What you can do is give me a chance to prove that who I am and what I do aren't the same thing. More than anyone else, you ought to understand. Who are you really? Midnight Mercy or Mercy May? What you do isn't who you are."

She closed her eyes and fought for control again. His touch was so seductive. He was always so good with words, twisting everything until it made sense. Pulling away from him, she brushed a hand across her wet eyes and paced. "Nick, what I do is make-believe. What you do is real. It's not the same."

"Sure it is, *chère*. Almost everything about my life until I met you was make-believe. After my parents and Catherine were killed, I didn't have the guts to practice real medicine, so I chose emergency medicine. I didn't have to give away a piece of my soul to every patient." His voice hardened. "God forbid that I should let myself feel something real, that I should let myself care for someone beyond the generic caring of one unknown human being to another."

Abruptly, Mercy stopped her pacing. The self-damnation in Nick's voice captured her complete attention, and he didn't even know it. He was sitting on the staircase staring at his clasped hands, forcing himself to continue.

"And then I met you. The pretending got harder after that. And tonight, for the first time, it was impossible. You see, *chère*, in emergency medicine, the injury is supposed to be the important thing. You do the best you can, and you walk away. Only tonight I couldn't walk away. I keep thinking about the thirteen-year-old kid I couldn't save. A kid who was named Tommy, had braces, and played the trombone . . . that he was proud of his blue ribbon . . . that he grabbed my hand and wouldn't let go." Finally he looked up. "And I knew I couldn't pretend not to care anymore. No matter how much it hurt."

Nick's pain was real, so real Mercy could feel it in every pore of her body. His knuckles were white from how tightly he clasped his hands, as if he were forcing himself to tell her everything. When he ran a hand across his face, taking a deep breath, she tensed. Instinctively, she knew the worst was yet to come.

Pulling the gold chain out of his shirt, Nick rubbed the medallion between his thumb and forefinger. "I was fifteen years old when my sister was born. This was Catherine's, a gift from me the day she started school. She wore it every day for two years."

"Patron saint of children," Mercy said, closing her eyes against the wave of uneasiness that flowed over her. When she opened them, she had somehow moved closer to Nick. Close enough to touch his shoulder in support if she wanted. And she wanted to. She wanted to sit down beside him and tell him it didn't matter anymore. That she didn't need to hear this. But she didn't. She let him say what he needed to say.

"Yeah, patron saint of children and the patron saint of travelers. Catherine gave it back to me the day I left for medical school. She thought I needed it more." Nick shoved himself up from the stairs and walked away from her. "She and my parents were killed in a boating accident the next day. She was eight years old, and it tore my heart out. A voice on a phone regretted to inform me that my world had just been blown apart."

"Oh, my God."

He turned and continued as if Mercy hadn't said anything. "I raised Catherine just as much as my parents did. I walked the floor when she was sick. I held her hand when she needed a big brother. See, *chère*, before I met you, I knew all about heartbreak. I knew all about caring. The one thing I don't know was the people who come through my emergency room. If I did, then I'd have cared, and I couldn't care about them. I couldn't let them tear my heart out every day."

Mercy was crying again, this time for Nick's pain. She took a step closer, but Nick stopped her from reaching out with a shake of his head. He wasn't finished.

"You were right about me. I tried to turn off my emotions. I didn't want to know too much. Every time a patient died, I didn't want to carry them with me. I didn't want to think of Catherine dying all alone. I didn't want to think of losing the people I loved. I even managed to pretend for a while. But I can't anymore. I can't because I'm in love with you. You brought me back to life somehow."

Mercy's heart thumped heavily against her chest and any thought she had of walking away from this man vanished. As Nick extended his hand she let him pull her close.

"I wear this medallion because I can't let go of the people I love. You're one of those people, *chère*.

I want to marry you. I'm not going anywhere. You should have believed me when I told you I wasn't near through with you. And never will be. Nothing you can do is going to change the way I feel or make me disappear."

All of her doubts vanished. Knowing that everything she wanted was hers, Mercy tried not to cry as she said, "How could I make you disappear? I can't even make you take no for an answer."

"Then say yes."

"Yes."

"Now say I love you."

Her eyes shining, Mercy repeated, "I love you, Nicholas Octave Devereaux."

"*Mais yeah, chère.* Let me show you how we seal an engagement on the bayou."

Mercy laughed as he slung her over his shoulder in a credible caveman imitation and carried her up the stairs. When he deposited her on the bed, Mercy told him, "You know we have to tell Sophie first. She'll never forgive me if she hears it somewhere else."

"Darlin', she knew it before we did. She's already got her mother-of-the-bride dress all picked out. Now kiss me."

"With pleasure."

THE EDITOR'S CORNER

Along with the May flowers come six fabulous Loveswepts that will dazzle you with humor, excitement, and, above all, love. Touching, tender, packed with emotion and wonderfully happy endings, our six upcoming romances are real treasures.

The ever-popular Charlotte Hughes leads things off with **THE DEVIL AND MISS GOODY TWO-SHOES**, LOVESWEPT #684. Kane Stoddard had never answered the dozens of letters Melanie Abercrombie had written him in prison, but her words had kept his spirit alive during the three years he'd been jailed in error—and now he wants nothing more than a new start, and a chance to meet the woman who touched his angry soul. Stunned by the sizzling attraction she feels for Kane, Mel struggles to deny the passionate emotions Kane's touch awakens. No one had ever believed in Kane until Mel's sweet caring makes him dare to taste her innocent lips, makes him hunger to hold her until the sun rises. He can only hope that his fierce loving will vanquish her fear of losing him. Touching and intense, **THE DEVIL AND MISS GOODY TWO-SHOES** is the kind of love story that Charlotte is known and loved for.

This month Terry Lawrence delivers some **CLOSE ENCOUNTERS**, LOVESWEPT #685—but of the romantic kind. Alone in the elevator with his soon-to-be ex-wife, Tony Paretti decides he isn't giving Sara Cohen up without a fight! But when fate sends the elevator plunging ten floors and tosses her into his arms, he seizes his chance—and with breath-stealing abandon embraces the woman he's never stopped loving. Kissing Sara with a savage passion that transcends pain, Tony insists that what they had was too good to let go, that together they are strong enough to face the grief that shattered their marriage. Sara aches to rebuild the bonds of their love but doesn't know if she can trust him with her sorrow, even after Tony confesses the secret hopes that he's never dared to tell another soul. Terry will have you crying and cheering as these two people discover the courage to love again.

Get ready for a case of mistaken identity in **THE ONE FOR ME**, LOVESWEPT #686, by Mary Kay McComas. It was a ridiculous masquerade, pretending to be his twin brother at a business dinner, but Peter Wesley grows utterly confused when his guest returns from the powder room—and promptly steals his heart! She looks astonishingly like the woman he'd dined with earlier, but he's convinced that the cool fire and passionate longing in her bright blue eyes is new and dangerously irresistible. Katherine Asher hates impersonating her look-alike sisters, and seeing Peter makes her regret she'd ever agreed. When he kisses her with primitive yearning, she aches to admit her secret—that she wants him for herself! Once the charade is revealed, Peter woos her with fierce pleasure until she surrenders. She has always taken her happiness last, but is she ready to put her love for him first? **THE ONE FOR ME** is humorous and hot—just too good to resist.

Marcia Evanick gives us a hero who is **PLAYING FOR KEEPS**, LOVESWEPT #687. For the past two years detective Reece Carpenter has solved the fake murder-mystery at the Montgomery clan's annual family reunion, infuriating the beautiful—and competitive—Tennessee Montgomery. But when he faces his tempting rival this time, all he wants to win is her heart! Tennie has come prepared to beat her nemesis if it kills her—but the wild flames in his eyes light a fire in her blood that only his lips can satisfy. Tricked into working as a team, Tennie and Reece struggle to prove which is the better sleuth, but the enforced closeness creates a bigger challenge: to keep their minds on the case when they can't keep their hands off each other! Another keeper from Marcia Evanick.

STRANGE BEDFELLOWS, LOVESWEPT #688, is the newest wonderful romance from Patt Bucheister. John Lomax gave up rescuing ladies in distress when he traded his cop's mean streets for the peace of rural Kentucky, but he feels his resolve weaken when he discovers Silver Knight asleep on his couch! Her sea nymph's eyes brimming with delicious humor, her temptress's smile teasingly seductive, Silver pleads with him to probe a mystery in her New York apartment—and her hunk of a hero is hooked! Fascinated by her reluctant knight, an enigmatic warrior whose pain only she can soothe, Silver wonders if a joyous romp might help her free his spirit from the demons of a shadowy past. He is her reckless gamble, the dare she can't refuse—but she needs to make him understand his true home is in her arms. **STRANGE BEDFELLOWS** is Patt Bucheister at her sizzling best.

And last, but certainly not least, is **NO PROMISES MADE**, LOVESWEPT #689, by Maris Soule. Eric Newman is a sleek black panther of a man who holds Ashley Kehler spellbound, mesmerizing her with a look that strips her bare and caresses her senses, but he could also make her lose control, forget the dreams that drive her . . . and Ashley knows she must resist this seducer who ignites a fever in her blood! Drawn to this golden spitfire who is his opposite in every way, Eric feels exhilarated, intrigued against his will—but devastated by the knowledge that she'll soon be leaving. Ashley wavers between ecstasy and guilt, yet Eric knows the only way to keep his love is to let her go, hoping that she is ready to choose the life that will bring her joy. Don't miss this fabulous story!

Happy reading!

With warmest wishes,

Nita Taublib

Nita Taublib
Associate Publisher

P.S. Don't miss the exciting women's novels from Bantam that are coming your way in May—**DECEPTION**, by Amanda Quick, is the paperback edition of her first *New York Times* bestselling hardcover; **RELENTLESS**, by award-winning author Patricia Potter, is a searing tale of revenge and desire, set in Colorado during the 1870's; **SEIZED BY LOVE**, by Susan Johnson, is a novel of savage passions and dangerous pleasures sweeping from fabulous country estates and hunting lodges to the opulent ballrooms and salons of Russian nobility; and **WILD CHILD**, by bestselling author Suzanne Forster, reunites adversaries who share a tangled past—and for whom an old spark of conflict will kindle into a dangerously passionate blaze. We'll be giving you a sneak peek at these terrific books in next month's LOVESWEPTs. And immediately following this page look for a preview of the exciting romances from Bantam that are *available now*!

Don't miss these exciting books by your
favorite Bantam authors

On sale in March:

DARK PARADISE
by Tami Hoag

WARRIOR BRIDE
by Tamara Leigh

REBEL IN SILK
by Sandra Chastain

"Ms. Hoag has deservedly become one of the romance genre's most treasured authors."
—*Rave Reviews*

Look For

DARK PARADISE
by
Tami Hoag

Here is nationally bestselling author Tami Hoag's most dangerously erotic novel yet, a story filled with heart-stopping suspense and shocking passion . . . a story of a woman drawn to a man as hard and untamable as the land he loves, and to a town steeped in secrets—where a killer lurks.

Night had fallen by the time Mari finally found her way to Lucy's place with the aid of the map Lucy had sent in her first letter. Her "hide-out," she'd called it. The huge sky was as black as velvet, sewn with the sequins of more stars than she had ever imagined. The world suddenly seemed a vast, empty wilderness, and she pulled into the yard of the small ranch, questioning for the first time the wisdom of a surprise arrival. There were no lights glowing a welcome in the windows of the handsome new log house. The garage doors were closed.

She climbed out of her Honda and stretched, feeling exhausted and rumpled. The past two weeks had sapped her strength, the decisions she had made taking chunks of it at a time. The drive up from Sacramento had been accomplished in a twenty-four hour marathon with breaks for nothing more than the bathroom and truck stop burritos, and now the physical strain of that weighed her down like an anchor.

It had seemed essential that she get here as quickly as possible, as if she had been afraid her nerve would give out and she would succumb to the endless dissatisfaction of her life in California if she didn't escape immediately. The wild pendulum her emotions had been riding had left her feeling drained and dizzy. She had counted on falling into Lucy's care the instant she got out of her car, but Lucy didn't appear to be home, and disappointment sent the pendulum swinging downward again.

Foolish, really, she told herself, blinking back the threat of tears as she headed for the front porch. She couldn't have expected Lucy to know she was coming. She hadn't been able to bring herself to call ahead. A call would have meant an explanation of everything that had gone on in the past two weeks, and that was better made in person.

A calico cat watched her approach from the porch rail, but jumped down and ran away as she climbed the steps, its claws scratching the wood floor as it darted around the corner of the porch and disappeared. The wind swept down off the mountain and howled around the weathered outbuildings, bringing with it a sense of isolation and a vague feeling of desertion that Mari tried to shrug off as she raised a hand and knocked on the door.

No lights brightened the windows. No voice called out for her to keep her pants on.

She swallowed at the combination of disappointment and uneasiness that crowded at the back of her throat. Against her will, her eyes did a quick scan of the moon-shadowed ranch yard and the hills beyond. The place was in the middle of nowhere. She had driven through the small town of New Eden and gone miles into the wilderness, seeing no more than two other houses on the way—and those from a great distance.

She knocked again, but didn't wait for an answer before trying the door. Lucy had mentioned wildlife in her few letters. The four-legged, flea-scratching kind.

"Bears. I remember something about bears," she muttered, the nerves at the base of her neck wriggling at the possibility that there were a dozen watching her from the cover of darkness, sizing her up with their beady little eyes while their stomachs growled. "If it's all the same to you, Luce, I'd rather not meet one up close and personal while you're off doing the boot scootin' boogie with some cowboy."

Stepping inside, she fumbled along the wall for a light switch, then blinked against the glare of a dozen small bulbs artfully arranged in a chandelier of antlers. Her first thought was that Lucy's abysmal housekeeping talents had deteriorated to a shocking new low. The place was a disaster area, strewn with books, newspapers, note paper, clothing.

She drifted away from the door and into the great room that encompassed most of the first floor of the house, her brain stumbling to make sense of the contradictory information it was getting. The house was barely a year old, a blend of Western tradition and contemporary architectural touches. Lucy had hired a decorator to capture those intertwined feelings in the interior. But the western watercolor prints on the walls hung at drunken angles. The cushions had been torn from the heavy, overstuffed chairs. The seat of the red leather sofa had been slit from end to end. Stuffing rose up from the wound in ragged tufts. Broken lamps and shattered pottery littered the expensive Berber rug. An overgrown pothos had been ripped from its planter and shredded, and was strung across the carpet like strips of tattered green ribbon.

Not even Lucy was this big a slob.

Mari's pulse picked up the rhythm of fear. "Lucy?" she called, the tremor in her voice a vocal extension of the goosebumps that were pebbling her arms. The only answer was an ominous silence that pressed in on her eardrums until they were pounding.

She stepped over a gutted throw pillow, picked her way around a smashed terra cotta urn and peered into the darkened kitchen area. The refrigerator door was ajar, the light within glowing like the promise of gold inside a treasure chest. The smell, however, promised something less pleasant.

She wrinkled her nose and blinked against the sour fumes as she found the light switch on the wall and flicked it upward. Recessed lighting beamed down on a repulsive mess of spoiling food and spilled beer. Milk puddled on the Mexican tile in front of the refrigerator. The carton lay abandoned on its side. Flies hovered over the garbage like tiny vultures.

"Jesus, Lucy," she muttered, "what kind of party did you throw here?"

And where the hell are you?

The pine cupboard doors stood open, their contents spewed out of them. Stoneware and china and flatware lay broken and scattered. Appropriately macabre place settings for the gruesome meal that had been laid out on the floor.

Mari backed away slowly, her hand trembling as she reached out to steady herself with the one ladder-back chair that remained upright at the long pine harvest table. She caught her full lower lip between her teeth and stared through the sheen of tears. She had worked too many criminal cases not to see this for what it was. The house had been ransacked. The motive could have been robbery or the destruction could have been the aftermath of something else, something uglier.

"Lucy?" she called again, her heart sinking like a stone at the sure knowledge that she wouldn't get an answer.

Her gaze drifted to the stairway that led up to the loft where the bedrooms were tucked, then cut to the telephone that had been ripped from the kitchen wall and now hung by slender tendons of wire.

Her heart beat faster. A fine mist of sweat slicked her palms.

"Lucy?"

"She's dead."

The words were like a pair of shotgun blasts in the still of the room. Mari wheeled around, a scream wedged in her throat right behind her heart. He stood at the other end of the table, six feet of hewn granite in faded jeans and a chambray work shirt. How anything that big could have sneaked up on her was beyond reasoning. Her perceptions distorted by fear, she thought his shoulders rivaled the mountains for size. He stood there, staring at her from beneath the low-riding brim of a dusty black Stetson, his gaze narrow, measuring, his mouth set in a grim, compressed line. His right hand—big with blunt-tipped fingers—hung at his side just inches from a holstered revolver that looked big enough to bring down a buffalo.

WARRIOR BRIDE
by
Tamara Leigh

"*. . . a vibrant, passionate love story that captures all the splendor of the medieval era . . . A sheer delight.*"
— *bestselling author Teresa Medeiros*

After four years of planning revenge on the highway-man who'd stolen her future, Lizanne Balmaine had the blackguard at the point of her sword. Yet some-thing about the onyx-eyed man she'd abducted and taken to her family estate was different—something that made her hesitate at her moment of triumph. Now she was his prisoner . . . and even more than her handsome captor she feared her own treacherous desires.

"Welcome, my Lord Ranulf," she said. "'Tis a fine day for a duel."

He stared unblinkingly at her, then let a frown settle between his eyes. "Forsooth, I did not expect you to attend this bloodletting," he said. "I must needs remember you are not a lady."

Her jaw hardened. "I assure you I would not miss this for anything," she tossed back.

He looked at the weapons she carried. "And where is this man who would champion your ill-fated cause?" he asked, looking past her.

"Man?" She shook her head. "There is no man."

Ranulf considered this, one eyebrow arched. "You were unable to find a single man willing to die for you, my lady? Not one?"

Refusing to rise to the bait, Lizanne leaned forward, smiling faintly. "Alas, I fear I am so uncomely that none would offer."

"And what of our bargain?" Ranulf asked, suspicion cast upon his voice.

"It stands."

"You think to hold me till your brother returns?" He shifted more of his weight onto his uninjured leg. "Do you forget that I am an unwilling captive, my lady? 'Tis not likely you will return me to that foul-smelling cell." He took a step toward her.

At his sudden movement, the mare shied away, snorting loudly as it pranced sideways. Lizanne brought the animal under control with an imperceptible tightening of her legs.

"Nay," she said, her eyes never wavering. "Your opponent is here before you now."

Ranulf took some moments to digest this, then burst out laughing. As preposterous as it was, a mere woman challenging an accomplished knight to a duel of swords, her proposal truly did not surprise him, though it certainly amused him.

And she was not jesting! he acknowledged. Amazingly, it fit the conclusions he had wrestled with, and finally accepted, regarding her character.

Had she a death wish, then? Even if that spineless brother of hers had shown her how to swing a sword, it was inconceivable she could have any proficiency with such a heavy, awkward weapon. A sling, perhaps, and he mustn't forget a dagger, but a sword?

Slowly, he sobered, blinking back tears of mirth and drawing deep, ragged breaths of air.

She edged her horse nearer, her indignation evident in her stiffly erect bearing. "I find no humor in the situation. Mayhap you would care to enlighten me, Lord Ranulf?"

"Doubtless, you would not appreciate my explanation, my lady."

Her chin went up. "Think you I will not make a worthy opponent?"

"With your nasty tongue, perhaps, but—"

"Then let us not prolong the suspense any longer," she snapped. Swiftly, she removed the sword from its scabbard and tossed it, hilt first, to him.

Reflexively, Ranulf pulled it from the air, his hand closing around the cool metal hilt. He was taken aback as he held it aloft, for inasmuch as the weapon appeared perfectly honed on both its edges, it was not the weighty sword he was accustomed to. Indeed, it felt awkward in his grasp.

"And what is this, a child's toy?" he quipped, twisting the sword in his hand.

In one fluid motion, Lizanne dismounted and turned to face him. "'Tis the instrument of your death, my lord." Advancing, she drew her own sword, identical to the one he held.

He lowered his sword's point and narrowed his eyes. "Think you I would fight a woman?"

"'Tis as we agreed."

"I agreed to fight a man—"

"Nay, you agreed to fight the opponent of my choice. I stand before you now ready to fulfill our bargain."

"We have no such bargain," he insisted.

"Would you break your vow? Are you so dishonorable?"

Never before had Ranulf's honor been questioned. For King Henry and, when necessary, himself, he had fought hard and well, and he carried numerous battle scars to attest to his valor. Still, her insult rankled him.

"'Tis honor that compels me to decline," he

said, a decidedly dangerous smile playing about his lips.

"Honor?" She laughed, coming to an abrupt halt a few feet from him. "Methinks 'tis your injury, coward. Surely, you can still wield a sword?"

Coward? A muscle in his jaw jerked. This one was expert at stirring the remote depths of his anger. "Were you a man, you would be dead now."

"Then imagine me a man," she retorted, lifting her sword in challenge.

The very notion was laughable. Even garbed as she was, the Lady Lizanne was wholly a woman.

"Nay, I fear I must decline." Resolutely, he leaned on the sword. "'Twill make a fine walking stick, though," he added, flexing the steel blade beneath his weight.

Ignoring his quip, Lizanne took a step nearer. "You cannot decline!"

"Aye, and I do."

"Then I will gut you like a pig!" she shouted and leaped forward.

REBEL IN SILK
by
Sandra Chastain

*"Sandra Chastain's characters' steamy relationships
are the stuff dreams are made of."*
—Romantic Times

*Dallas Burke had come to Willow Creek, Wyoming,
to find her brother's killer, and she had no intention of being scared off—not by the roughnecks who
trashed her newspaper office, nor by the devilishly
handsome cowboy who warned her of the violence to
come. Yet she couldn't deny that the tall, sunbronzed
rancher had given her something to think about,
namely, what it would be like to be held in his
steel-muscled arms and feel his sensuous mouth on
hers . . . .*

A bunch of liquored-up cowboys were riding past
the station, shooting guns into the air, bearing down
on the startled Miss Banning caught by drifts in the
middle of the street.

From the general store, opposite where Dallas
was standing, came a figure who grabbed her valise
in one hand and scooped her up with the other, flung her over his shoulder, and stepped onto
the wooden sidewalk beneath the roof over the
entrance to the saloon.

Dallas let out a shocked cry as the horses
thundered by. She might have been run over had
it not been for the man's quick action. Now,
hanging upside down, she felt her rescuer's hand

cradling her thigh in much too familiar a manner.

"Sir, what are you doing?"

"Saving your life."

The man lifted her higher, then, as she started to slide, gave her bottom another tight squeeze. Being rescued was one thing, but this was out of line. Gratitude flew out of her mind as he groped her backside.

"Put me down, you . . . you . . . lecher!"

"Gladly!" He leaned forward, loosened his grip and let her slide to the sidewalk where she landed in a puddle of melted snow and ice. The valise followed with a thump.

"Well, you didn't have to try to break my leg!" Dallas scrambled to her feet, her embarrassment tempering her fear and turning it into anger.

"No, I could have let the horses do it!"

Dallas had never heard such cold dispassion in a voice. He wasn't flirting with her. He wasn't concerned about her injuries. She didn't know why he'd bothered to touch her so intimately. One minute he was there, and the next he had turned to walk away.

"Wait, please wait! I'm sorry to appear ungrateful. I was just startled."

As she scurried along behind him, all she could see was the hat covering his face and head, his heavy canvas duster, and boots with silver spurs set with turquoise. He wasn't stopping.

Dallas reached out and caught his arm. "Now, just a minute. Where I come from, a man at least gives a lady the chance to say a proper thank you. What kind of man are you?"

"I'm cold, I'm thirsty, and I'm ready for a woman. Are you volunteering?"

There was a snickering sound that ran through the room they'd entered. Dallas raised her head and glanced around. She wasn't the only woman in the saloon, but she was the only one wearing all her clothes.

Any other woman might have gasped. But Dallas suppressed her surprise. She didn't know the layout of the town yet, and until she did, she wouldn't take a chance of offending anyone, even these ladies of pleasure. "I'm afraid not. I'm a newspaperwoman, not a . . . an entertainer."

He ripped his hat away, shaking off the glistening beads of melting snow that hung in the jet-black hair that touched his shoulders. He was frowning at her, his brow drawn into deep lines of displeasure; his lips, barely visible beneath a bushy mustache, pressed into a thin line.

His eyes, dark and deep, held her. She sensed danger and a hot intensity.

Where the man she'd met on the train seemed polished and well-mannered, her present adversary was anything but a gentleman. He was a man of steel who challenged with every glance. She shivered in response.

"Hello," a woman's voice intruded. "I'm Miranda. You must have come in on the train."

Dallas blinked, breaking the contact between her and her rescuer. With an effort, she turned to the woman.

"Ah, yes. I did. Dallas Banning." She started to hold out her hand, realized that she was clutching her valise, then lowered it. "I'm afraid I've made rather a mess of introducing myself to Green Willow Creek."

"Well, I don't know about what happened in the street, but following Jake in here might give your reputation a bit of a tarnish."

"Jake?" This was the Jake that her brother Jamie had been worried about.

"Why, yes," Miranda said, "I assumed you two knew each other?"

"Not likely," Jake growled and turned to the bar. "She's too skinny and her mouth is too big for my taste."

"Miss Banning?" Elliott Parnell, the gentleman she'd met on the train, rushed in from the street. "I saw what happened. Are you all right?"

Jake looked up, catching Dallas between him and the furious look he cast at Elliott Parnell.

Dallas didn't respond. The moment Jake had spotted Mr. Elliott, everything in the saloon had seemed to stop. All movement. All sound. For a long endless moment it seemed as if everyone in the room were frozen in place.

Jake finally spoke. "If she's with you and your sodbusters, Elliott, you'd better get her out of here."

Elliot took Dallas's arm protectively. "No, Jake. We simply came in on the same train. Miss Banning is James Banning's sister."

"Oh? The troublemaking newspaper editor. Almost as bad as the German immigrants. I've got no use for either one. Take my advice, Miss Banning. Get on the next train back to wherever you came from."

"I don't need your advice, Mr. Silver."

"Suit yourself, but somebody didn't want your brother here, and my guess is that you won't be any more welcome!"

Dallas felt a shiver of pure anger ripple down her backbone. She might as well make her position known right now. She came to find out the truth and she wouldn't be threatened. "Mr. Silver—"

"Jake! Elliott!" Miranda interrupted, a warning in her voice. "Can't you see that Miss Banning is half-frozen? Men! You have to forgive them," she said, turning to Dallas. "At the risk of further staining your reputation, I'd be pleased to have you make use of my room to freshen up and get dry. That is if you don't mind being . . . here."

"I'd be most appreciative, Miss Miranda," Dallas said, following her golden-haired hostess to the stairs.

Dallas felt all the eyes in the room boring holes in her back. She didn't have to be told where she was and what was taking place beyond the doors on either side of the corridor. If being here ruined her reputation, so be it. She wasn't here to make friends anyway. Besides, a lead to Jamie's murderer was a lot more likely to come from these people than those who might be shocked by her actions.

For just a second she wondered what would have happened if Jake had marched straight up the stairs with her. Then she shook off the impossible picture that thought had created.

She wasn't here to be bedded.

She was here to kill a man.

She just had to find out which one.

And don't miss these spectacular
romances from Bantam Books,
on sale in April:

DECEPTION
by the New York Times bestselling author
Amanda Quick
"One of the hottest and most
prolific writers in romance today . . ."
—*USA Today*

RELENTLESS
by the highly acclaimed author
Patricia Potter
"One of the romance genre's
finest talents . . ."
—*Romantic Times*

SEIZED BY LOVE
by the mistress of erotic historical romance
Susan Johnson
"Susan Johnson is one of the best."
—*Romantic Times*

WILD CHILD
by the bestselling author
Suzanne Forster
"(Suzanne Forster) is guaranteed to steam up
your reading glasses."
—*L.A. Daily News*

OFFICIAL RULES

To enter the sweepstakes below carefully follow all instructions found elsewhere in this offer.

The **Winners Classic** will award prizes with the following approximate maximum values: 1 Grand Prize: $26,500 (or $25,000 cash alternate); 1 First Prize: $3,000; 5 Second Prizes: $400 each; 35 Third Prizes: $100 each; 1,000 Fourth Prizes: $7.50 each. Total maximum retail value of Winners Classic Sweepstakes is $42,500. Some presentations of this sweepstakes may contain individual entry numbers corresponding to one or more of the aforementioned prize levels. To determine the Winners, individual entry numbers will first be compared with the winning numbers preselected by computer. For winning numbers not returned, prizes will be awarded in random drawings from among all eligible entries received. Prize choices may be offered at various levels. If a winner chooses an automobile prize, all license and registration fees, taxes, destination charges and, other expenses not offered herein are the responsibility of the winner. If a winner chooses a trip, travel must be complete within one year from the time the prize is awarded. Minors must be accompanied by an adult. Travel companion(s) must also sign release of liability. Trips are subject to space and departure availability. Certain black-out dates may apply.

The following applies to the sweepstakes named above:

No purchase necessary. You can also enter the sweepstakes by sending your name and address to: P.O. Box 508, Gibbstown, N.J. 08027. Mail each entry separately. Sweepstakes begins 6/1/93. Entries must be received by 12/30/94. Not responsible for lost, late, damaged, misdirected, illegible or postage due mail. Mechanically reproduced entries are not eligible. All entries become property of the sponsor and will not be returned.

Prize Selection/Validations: Selection of winners will be conducted no later than 5:00 PM on January 28, 1995, by an independent judging organization whose decisions are final. Random drawings will be held at 1211 Avenue of the Americas, New York, N.Y. 10036. Entrants need not be present to win. Odds of winning are determined by total number of entries received. Circulation of this sweepstakes is estimated not to exceed 200 million. All prizes are guaranteed to be awarded and delivered to winners. Winners will be notified by mail and may be required to complete an affidavit of eligibility and release of liability which must be returned within 14 days of date on notification or alternate winners will be selected in a random drawing. Any prize notification letter or any prize returned to a participating sponsor, Bantam Doubleday Dell Publishing Group, Inc., its participating divisions or subsidiaries, or the independent judging organization as undeliverable will be awarded to an alternate winner. Prizes are not transferable. No substitution for prizes except as offered or as may be necessary due to unavailability, in which case a prize of equal or greater value will be awarded. Prizes will be awarded approximately 90 days after the drawing. All taxes are the sole responsibility of the winners. Entry constitutes permission (except where prohibited by law) to use winners' names, hometowns, and likenesses for publicity purposes without further or other compensation. Prizes won by minors will be awarded in the name of parent or legal guardian.

Participation: Sweepstakes open to residents of the United States and Canada, except for the province of Quebec. Sweepstakes sponsored by Bantam Doubleday Dell Publishing Group, Inc., (BDD), 1540 Broadway, New York, NY 10036. Versions of this sweepstakes with different graphics and prize choices will be offered in conjunction with various solicitations or promotions by different subsidiaries and divisions of BDD. Where applicable, winners will have their choice of any prize offered at level won. Employees of BDD, its divisions, subsidiaries, advertising agencies, independent judging organization, and their immediate family members are not eligible.

Canadian residents, in order to win, must first correctly answer a time limited arithmetical skill testing question. Void in Puerto Rico, Quebec and wherever prohibited or restricted by law. Subject to all federal, state, local and provincial laws and regulations. For a list of major prize winners (available after 1/29/95): send a self-addressed, stamped envelope entirely separate from your entry to: Sweepstakes Winners, P.O. Box 517, Gibbstown, NJ 08027. Requests must be received by 12/30/94. DO NOT SEND ANY OTHER CORRESPONDENCE TO THIS P.O. BOX.